MONSTERIOUS

ESCAPE FROM GRIMSTONE MANOR

ALSO BY MATT McMANN

The Snatcher of Raven Hollow

MONSTERIOUS
ESCAPE FROM GRIMSTONE MANOR

MATT MCMANN

putnam

G. P. Putnam's Sons

G. P. Putnam's Sons
An imprint of Penguin Random House LLC, New York

First published in the United States of America by G. P. Putnam's Sons,
an imprint of Penguin Random House LLC, 2023

Copyright © 2023 by Matt McMann

Visit us online at PenguinRandomHouse.com.

Library of Congress Cataloging-in-Publication Data
Names: McMann, Matt, author. | Title: Escape from Grimstone Manor / Matt McMann.
Description: New York: G. P. Putnam's Sons, 2023. | Series: Monsterious
Summary: When a ride breaks down before closing, friends Mateo, Taylor, and Zari
find themselves stuck inside the haunted house for the night and discover a hidden
staircase leading to a dark crypt. | Identifiers: LCCN 2022045285 (print)
LCCN 2022045286 (ebook) | ISBN 9780593530696 (hardcover)
ISBN 9780593530719 (trade paperback) | ISBN 9780593530702 (epub)
Subjects: CYAC: Amusement parks—Fictions. | Haunted places—Fiction.
Monsters—Fiction. | Friendship—Fiction. | Horror stories. | Horror stories. lcgft
LCGFT: Novels. | Classification: LCC PZ7.1.M4636 Es 2023 (print)
LCC PZ7.1.M4636 (ebook) | DDC [Fic]—dc23
LC record available at https://lccn.loc.gov/2022045285
LC ebook record available at https://lccn.loc.gov/2022045286

Printed in the United States of America

ISBN 9780593530696 (hardcover)

ISBN 9780593530719 (paperback)

1st Printing
LSCC

Design by Nicole Rheingans
Text set in Maxime Pro

To my wife, Lisa, for paving the way

and believing I could follow

CHAPTER 1

"NO WAY," Mateo said, his arms crossed firmly over his chest. "I don't want nightmares for a week, thanks."

"Oh, don't be so dramatic," said Taylor, rolling her eyes. "It's just a *ride*."

"Grimstone Manor isn't 'just a ride,'" Mateo said. "It's more like a torture device."

Taylor turned to Zari with an exasperated sigh. "Will you please tell him he's being ridiculous?

And hurry up. It's already dark, and the park is closing soon."

"Um . . ." Zari bit her lip. Their arguments made her skin itch, and she hated being stuck in the middle. Turning to Mateo, she said, "I'll go. You can sit this one out."

Mateo looked conflicted, his thick brown hair framing his face in an artful mop since he'd discovered hair paste. Finally, he dropped his arms with a sigh. "Fine. Let's get this over with."

The three friends weaved through the crowd at ThrillVille, their local amusement park. Far ahead, the outline of a Gothic mansion appeared over a thick stand of trees. Soon they came to a moss-covered archway built with fake stones and displaying the words *Grimstone Manor* in creepy-looking letters. Gargoyle statues perched on either side of the arch, their tongues jutting out between blunted fangs. Simulated lightning flashed above twisted trees as chest-rattling thunder rumbled through hidden speakers.

Mateo's eyes widened. "I'm going to regret this."

"Don't worry," Zari said, patting his arm. "Taylor will fight the monsters for us."

They hurried through the archway to join the line. A bored-looking attendant pulled a chain across the opening behind them. "Just made it," he said, like he wished they hadn't. "Last ride of the night."

"Yes!" Taylor said, flicking her blond ponytail. "Today has been awesome. I'm *so* glad we pulled this off."

Mateo frowned. "I don't like that I lied to my dad about where we'd be."

"You didn't *lie*, exactly," Taylor said. "You just didn't update him on our change of plans."

"Like Zari and I didn't 'update' our parents that your mom and dad are out of town?" he said.

"They'd never have let us sleep at your place tonight if they'd known we'd be alone."

"We all went along with it, so let's not argue," Zari said.

Mateo gave a reluctant nod. In the distance, Grimstone Manor sat on a low hill, bathed in eerie green light, looking like a demented frog. He eyed the simulated swamp they'd have to cross before reaching the mansion. "The house is bad enough. Did they really have to add a scary swamp?"

"Just focus on that popcorn smell," Taylor said, drawing in a deep breath. "Zari will buy us some after the ride."

Zari laughed. "You wish." As the line crawled forward, she gazed up at the sinister-looking mansion. "I wonder if that's what the original house looked like."

"What original house?" asked Mateo.

"Hezekiah Crawly's mansion," she said. "You know, the one the ride is based on."

"Who's Hezekiah Crawly?" asked Mateo.

"Seriously?" Taylor said, giving him an astonished look. Then her expression relaxed. "Oh right, you didn't grow up here. You don't know all the boring local history stuff."

Zari gave an affronted sniff. "Boring? You call the legend of a missing necromancer boring?"

"A necro-whoser?" Mateo asked.

"Necro*mancer*," Zari said. "Someone who studies dark magic."

"So this Hezekiah guy was one of those?" Mateo asked.

"That's the legend," Zari said. "About a hundred years ago, Hezekiah Crawly lived in a mansion that stood right where the ride is now. There were rumors that he was really into dark magic, even stealing bodies from a local graveyard to try and raise the dead."

Mateo shivered. "Why would anyone *want* to raise the dead?"

"According to the rhyme, he wanted to rule the world," Taylor said.

"What rhyme?" Mateo asked.

"Oooh, come on, Zar, let's do the clapping with it!" Taylor said, moving to stand opposite Zari. They clapped their hands together in a rhythmic pattern as they chanted:

In a mansion on a hill
Lived a man no one could kill
Raised the dead with magic dark
To rule the world and make his mark
Disappeared but made his fame
Hezekiah was his name

As they finished, Taylor and Zari fell against each other in a fit of laughter.

"Want us to teach it to you?" Taylor asked Mateo when she'd caught her breath.

Mateo smirked. "I think I'll pass."

They finally reached the front of the line and entered a replica of a broken-down boathouse. As they stepped inside, a rolling fog tickled their ankles. Overhead, huge fake bats with red beady eyes hung from the rafters. Eerie groans and strange whispers seemed to come from all directions, mingling with sound effects of crickets, bullfrogs, and lapping water. Through the open front of the boathouse, Zari spied the gloomy mansion rising from the mist across the swamp. Her smile faded as she tugged nervously at one of her close-cropped coils.

Beside them on the water sat a small flat-bottomed boat. At the back stood a figure draped in ragged brown robes and holding a long pole. Glowing green eyes shone from the darkness beneath its hood. Then a spotlight flicked on, illuminating the figure's face. Or . . . *lack* of face. A yellowed skull grinned out at them.

"Gah!" Mateo said, turning away with a sharp breath.

"Who dares seek passage to Grimstone Manor?" said the skeleton, its jaw moving stiffly in time with the voice recording. "You must be brave . . . or foolish! To reach the manor, you must cross the perilous Swamp of Dread. If you succeed, you'll be welcomed by the inhabitants of the mansion. They *love* having guests for dinner . . . served medium-rare!" The skeleton pointed at them with a bony finger. "Exploring Grimstone Manor will require all your courage. Nasty surprises lurk around every corner. I'll see you after your journey . . . *if you survive!*"

With a final peal of crazed laughter, the spotlight faded and the skeleton fell silent.

An attendant, slouched on a stool against the wall, waved them forward without looking up from her phone. "No pictures or video recording allowed," she monotoned while pointing to an empty locker. "Place your cell phones in a locker and take the key. You'll pick them up afterward. Remain in the car at all times. Enjoy the ride."

They surrendered their phones and climbed into a waiting car. With a slight jerk, they left the boathouse and slid into the dimly lit swamp. Taylor whooped in excitement. Mateo looked nauseous.

"Come on, Matty. It's only a ride," Taylor said. "What could possibly happen?"

CHAPTER 2

THE CAR ran on a track hidden beneath the murky water. The three friends drifted slowly through patches of moonlight, gliding past sculpted trees that dangled twisted vines over their heads.

"What's that?" Mateo asked anxiously, pointing into the shadows, where a strange glow hovered above the water.

"A will-o'-the-wisp," Zari said. "It's a ghost that shines a light to fool travelers."

"And lead them to their *doom*!" said Taylor in a creepy voice. "Muahahaha!"

A huge snake dropped from a low branch and weaved hypnotically in front of them. Mateo managed not to scream while Taylor laughed and batted at its rubber head. Moments later, a long dark shape swam in front of the car, then disappeared.

"Was that a crocodile?" Mateo asked, his voice as tight as a bow string.

"Freshwater swamps have alligators," Zari said. "Crocs prefer salt water."

"Who cares?" Taylor said. "They're both cool."

With a huge spray of water, a giant alligator shot up beside the car, its animatronic jaws spread wide. Mateo screamed as the creature's red eyes flashed above rows of jagged teeth. With a violent shake of its massive head, the alligator snapped its jaws shut, then sank slowly beneath the surface.

"I'm going to get you back for this, Taylor," Mateo said, wringing water from his shirt.

"I know," she said, flashing him a cheeky grin.

Through the trees, soft lights shone from Grimstone Manor's tall windows. "We're almost there," Zari said.

A terrifying roar ripped through the darkness, making Mateo's scalp tingle. His knuckles were white as he clenched his seat. A moment later, they heard something wading toward them, sending waves splashing unnervingly against the side of the car. Taylor peered expectantly at thick vines hanging beneath the trees.

"Get out of the swamp, get out of the swamp, get out of the swamp," whispered Mateo, urging the car to hurry. He scooted forward on his seat as if to help it along.

The car stopped moving. A moment passed, then

two. Mateo whimpered in the silence. Abruptly, the curtain of vines beside them was swept aside.

Only an arm's length away stood a hulking swamp creature. It was seven feet tall and as wide as a house, covered in moss and coated with a slick layer of slime. The smell of rot and decay wafted over the friends as the creature glared at them with luminous green eyes.

The monster lunged. They screamed and shrank back as its tree-trunk arms swept over their heads, spraying them with water. As one clawed hand reached for Mateo, the car shot forward. The creature bounded after them, its long legs rapidly closing the distance. Mercifully, the car sped away. The monster gave up the chase with a menacing roar and slunk back into the swamp.

Taylor gave a whoop, her face glowing. "That was awesome! Really freaky."

"*Not* awesome," Mateo said. He held his head in his hands and looked ready to pass out.

The car reached a grassy bank and climbed up a track onto the mansion's lawn. Towering willow trees stood like silent sentinels on either side of the mansion, their branches drooping low over a prop cemetery. Scattered tombstones lay cracked and broken in the moonlight. As they passed slowly between creepy mausoleums, a howl rang out from beyond the willows.

"Ooh, it's a full moon tonight, Matty," said Taylor. "Sounds like the werewolves are out!"

"Hilarious," he said darkly.

"It'll all be over soon," Taylor said, turning sympathetic. While she loved needling Mateo, she stood up for him too. When she'd found out he was being harassed by Derrick Lawson last semester, she'd marched right up to the hulking bully and threatened to knock his teeth out. Zari had laughed to see Derrick cower by his locker in front of some-one half his size. Taylor was like a honey badger: small but fearless.

Grimstone Manor loomed above them, its towers casting a harsh silhouette against the star-filled sky. Shutters creaked ominously in the breeze. A broken-down railing lined a porch draped in shadow. The light from an upper window dimmed as a strange dark shape crossed behind the curtain. Zari's heart pounded as every detail of the manor screamed, *I'm haunted!*

Mateo muttered under his breath as the car tipped and climbed the mansion's wide steps, then paused before the massive front door. A gargoyle head with a ring through its hooked nose protruded from the wood, forming the world's ugliest door knocker. Its eyes snapped open and glowered at them.

"Who dares disturb my slumber?" the gargoyle said in a low, menacing voice. "More wanderers lost in the swamp? The master will not be pleased." The mechanical eyes slowly scanned their faces. "Then again, you do look . . . tasty. Perhaps the master will be glad to see you after all!"

With a loud creak, the door swung open, and the car jerked forward. The door slammed behind them, plunging them into darkness. It became eerily quiet. For a few moments, nothing happened. Taylor giggled in anticipation and poked Zari's side. Zari swatted her hand away.

Thunder boomed, and they all jumped. A lightning flash revealed a massive figure standing beside the car. Mateo's eyes swelled to the size of miniature waffles.

A lantern flared in the figure's beefy hand. It was a man . . . sort of. Not many men are eight feet tall. He had a distinctly "Frankenstein's monster" look about him, but wore a moldy butler's uniform, complete with a bow tie and a long-tailed coat. The glow from the lantern reflected off his pale green skin.

His mouth opened, and his voice was oily smooth.

"Welcome to Grimstone Manor."

CHAPTER 3

LIGHTS BLAZED in an iron chandelier, and the friends found themselves in a circular entrance hall. The walls were covered with a textured wallpaper featuring ghostly shapes soaring over dead trees. Beside the front door stood a wooden coatrack carved in the likeness of a rearing serpent. A table lamp with a multicolored glass shade sat between antique armchairs upholstered in blood-red velvet. Across the room, a curving staircase led to a second-floor landing lined with oil paintings of stern-looking people who glared down at them.

Zari shuddered. "I feel like we're in a horror movie."

"I know, isn't it awesome?" Taylor said.

"Did they really have to add a musty smell? Or is that . . . *him*?" Mateo asked, nervously eyeing the butler.

As if on cue, the man spoke again. "My master is unavailable at present. You may explore the house while you wait." His face creased in a ghastly smile. "But be warned. Grimstone Manor holds many surprises that will test your courage. Keep your wits about you. Farewell for now." The butler rotated in place and glided from the room.

"These animatronics are pretty impressive," Zari said.

"Yeah, I'd love to make monsters like that someday," Taylor said.

Zari arched an eyebrow. "You know you'd have to study mechanical engineering and computers, right?"

"I can handle all that," Taylor said, waving her hand dismissively. "Hey, we can be a team! I'll come up with the ideas, Mateo can draw the designs, and you can do all the boring stuff."

"Typical," Mateo murmured under his breath.

Their car spun to one side, then swept through a tall archway before stopping in a huge library. Floor-to-ceiling bookshelves lined the walls, each filled with leather-bound volumes that glowed in the light of brass floor lamps. A purple velvet couch sat under a window overlooking the moonlit cemetery. In a giant stone fireplace, flames flickered under a bubbling pot, sending shadows dancing around the room. Bobbing on the surface of the water were a pair of eyeballs, hairy ears, and a large, fleshy nose.

"Anyone hungry?" Zari asked weakly.

In one corner, a raven perched on an antique phonograph playing melancholy chamber music. With a harsh screech and a wild flapping of wings, the bird launched itself at the three friends. They ducked as the mechanical creature swept low over their heads and out of the library.

Mateo sat up grumbling. "Stupid bird."

They entered a dining room dominated by a long table filled with elaborate place settings. Fake cobwebs hung from a candelabra centerpiece. As their car stopped beside a large platter covered by a silver dome, a disembodied hand scuttled across the table like a terrifying crab. It snatched the dome from the platter, revealing a severed head that grinned out at them. Mateo turned away with a shudder.

The car wound slowly through the manor. They encountered a variety of animatronic monsters in a sitting room, a billiard room, a trophy room, and a kitchen. Jump scares made Mateo yelp and Taylor laugh.

In a back hallway, they came to a display cabinet holding glass jars filled with body parts and unidentifiable slimy things floating in clear liquid. The cabinet slid aside, revealing a secret opening. Their car turned and entered a hidden room filled with old books and bubbling beakers. Flickering light from dozens of fake candles cast eerie shadows. Against the far wall, an old man with ivory skin, wearing a black robe, stood behind a table, where a familiar shape lay wrapped in cream-colored strips of cloth.

"Wonderful," said Mateo. "A mummy."

The car stopped in front of the table, and the man in the robe came to life. His animatronic arms waved over the mummy as he spoke.

"De la morte à la vie! I, Hezekiah Crawly, will use my dark magic to raise an army of the living dead and rule the world!"

Taylor leaned over and whispered, "My pet tarantula's name is Hezekiah Crawly."

"Shh!" Zari said, but snorted into her hand.

The mummy twitched on the table, then slowly rose to a seated position. It turned its head and glared at them with glowing red eyes through a gap in its wrappings. Mateo shrank back, trying to get as far away as possible.

With a loud groan, the mummy lunged toward them. Just in time, the car shot in reverse, and the mummy's arms swept empty air. Once they were out in the hallway, the cabinet slid back across the opening.

"That last room really tracked with the Hezekiah rhyme," Taylor said as the ride continued.

"Still think local history is boring?" Zari asked, her eyebrow arching.

"Most of the time," Taylor said. "But the ghosty parts are cool. Right, Mateo?"

"I'm gonna go with no," he said weakly, his brown skin looking a shade paler than usual.

Their car tilted back and climbed the track up a wide staircase to the second floor. They entered a bedroom where an old woman in a pink nightgown lay on a canopy bed. She shot upright and cast a withering gaze at them with bulging green eyes beneath a wild tangle of white hair. Gray, leathery skin clung to her skull-like face. She pointed at them with a bony finger and shrieked, *"Get out of my room!"*

The car quickly reversed direction back into the hallway. They continued through two more bedrooms and an art gallery filled with nightmarish paintings. After exiting the gallery, their car stopped in the middle of a hallway lined with closed doors.

"Nooo," Mateo groaned. He flopped forward, then jerked up and looked around nervously. The seconds ticked by.

Taylor drummed her fingers on her knee.

"Something better leap out of one of these doors, or I want my money back."

"Wait a sec," Zari said, frowning at the car's front panel. "The dash lights are off."

"What do you mean?" Mateo asked anxiously. "Is something wrong with the car?"

"When we were stopped before, the power lights were always on," Zari said. "But this time they blinked, then turned off."

"Excellent!" said Taylor. "The ride broke down. Let's go explore!"

"Right," Zari said with a smirk.

"I'm serious," Taylor replied. "Rides break down all the time, and they always take forever to fix. We can look around for a few minutes, no problem."

"No way," Mateo said. "We're not going anywhere."

"Maybe *you're* not," Taylor said, unbuckling her seat belt.

"Seriously?" he said. "You know we're not supposed to leave the car."

Zari put her head in her hands.

"If a worker gets mad, we'll tell them we were looking for help," Taylor said. "Besides, we need to see behind the scenes if we want to build animatronics someday. When are we going to get another chance like this? Zari's always saying we should 'take advantage of educational opportunities' like she's thirty-five or whatever."

Taylor glanced around, then stepped out of the car.

Mateo looked at Zari. "Are you going to back me up here? You know she shouldn't be doing this."

"Um . . ." Zari said, nervously fidgeting with her coils. She agreed with Mateo but didn't want Taylor to get mad. "Maybe . . . I mean . . ."

Mateo rolled his eyes and turned back to Taylor. "Get in the car!"

"Relax. I'll be back before you know it." Taylor walked down the hall, jiggling door handles as she went. The third door opened. "Whoa, you've gotta see this!" she said, then disappeared through the doorway.

"Unbelievable," Mateo said. "Actually, totally believable. This *is* Taylor we're talking about. And thanks a lot for backing me up."

"I didn't . . ." Zari began, then sighed. She gazed down the cobwebbed hallway and called out, "Taylor, come on!" No response. After a few seconds, she unbuckled her seat belt.

"Whoa, what are you doing?" Mateo asked.

"Going after Taylor. I don't want to get in trouble because of her."

"But what about me?" he asked, his voice pitching higher.

"Stay here. I'll be right back."

Zari stepped out of the car and hurried through the door after Taylor. The painstakingly decorated Gothic mansion vanished. The room had a simple plywood floor and bare stud walls. It was cluttered with cables and machinery she didn't recognize, probably used to control the animatronics. A sign with large red letters hung on one wall: REMEMBER TO LOCK ALL DOORS!

"Irony," Zari muttered. Across the room, a low door stood open. "Taylor? Taylor!"

Silence.

With a sigh of frustration, Zari stepped toward the door just as something grabbed her shoulder.

She gasped and whirled to see Mateo standing behind her.

He gave a cry of fright. "Jeez, Zari, you scared me."

"You're the one who snuck up on me! What are you doing?"

"I got freaked out sitting there by myself. Is she in here?"

Taylor shook her head. "I think she went through that door."

"It figures. Let's hurry up. I want out of this creep show."

Crossing the room, they ducked through the low doorway and found themselves in an unfinished passage. Bare lightbulbs connected by drooping wires glowed dimly. At the far end, the friends came to a closed door. Zari opened it and stepped through.

"RAAHH!!" Taylor leaped from the shadows, making them both jump. Mateo fell on his butt with a shriek, which made Taylor double over with laughter.

"What the . . . !" Mateo sputtered. "You . . . you . . ."

"What's that, Matty?" Taylor said. "Ghost got your tongue?"

Zari glared at her friend. She felt like telling Taylor off, but bit her lip. Again.

"Not. Cool," Mateo spat. "Seriously."

When she saw his furious expression, Taylor's grin faded. "Sorry," she said, then reached down and helped him up. "Sometimes I can't help myself."

"*Try,*" Mateo growled.

"Let's get back to the car," Zari said, glancing around uneasily.

As they hurried along the passage, they heard a mechanical clattering sound. Zari's gut lurched, and she broke into a run, with Mateo and Taylor pounding along behind her. They raced through the machine room and entered the decorated hallway of the manor.

The car was gone.

CHAPTER 4

"OOPS," TAYLOR said.

"You think?" said Mateo.

"Come on!" Zari charged down the track after the missing car.

They rounded a corner and ran by mounted banshee heads with roving eyes. A huge animatronic yeti roared as they passed. One giant hand swept down and struck Mateo on the shoulder.

"Owww!" he yelled. "I hate this place!"

"It's motion controlled," Taylor called back. "It wouldn't have hit you if you were in the car."

"I wonder why I'm not?"

They rushed down the stairs. At the bottom, Taylor caught sight of their car rolling dutifully toward the front door, about to exit the ride. The creepy butler was saying some recorded message to the empty car that she couldn't make out.

"Aw, duckweed!" she yelled, then rushed down the dark hallway ahead of the others. "Hurry!"

Zari's foot caught on a display case full of withered hands, and she fell. Mateo plowed into her as she struggled to her feet, sending them both to the floor. Taylor reached the car and was about to climb in when she noticed her friends. Racing back, she pulled them up, and they all surged forward again.

It was too late. The car rolled onto the front porch, and the mansion's huge door slammed shut behind it.

Mateo sprinted to the door and tugged desperately at the handle.

"It's locked!" he said, breathing hard.

"Let me try." Zari examined the door, then gave the handle a sharp twist. When that didn't work, she jiggled it softly. No luck. "It's not made to be opened this way. It's all mechanical."

"Oh no," Mateo said in a panicked voice. "No, no, no way. We have to get out of here!"

"We *will*," Zari said, trying to stay calm. "There must be an emergency exit somewhere. We just have to find it."

"Cool!" Taylor said. "More exploring."

Mateo spun to face her. "Cool? No, *not* cool! This is *your* fault. Why do you always have to do stupid stuff like that!"

"Whoa," Taylor said, her blue eyes flashing. "Taking chances isn't stupid. It's called *living*. Not that you'd know. You're afraid of *everything*."

"I am not!"

"Are too," she said stubbornly, her hands on her hips.

"Come on, don't . . ." Zari said weakly.

Taylor crossed her arms defiantly at Mateo. "Nobody forced you to follow me. You did that on your own. Besides, if Zari hadn't tripped, we'd all be out of here right now."

"Hey!" Zari felt her temperature rising at Taylor's refusal to take any responsibility, not to mention the shot at her clumsiness. Taylor glared at them, and they glared back. The silent butler stood nearby, an odd fourth character in their little friendship drama. Zari loved Taylor's spontaneity, but Taylor didn't always think things through. She was right about not making them go after her, though. Zari sighed. "We did choose to follow you. Right, Mateo?"

He glowered at Taylor and didn't respond.

"I'll take that as a yes," Taylor said with a sniff.

"Fine," he said. "But you running off like that could have gotten *us* in trouble too. Like the time you decided to skateboard down the hall at school when we were supposed to be cleaning the trophy case."

Taylor grinned. "The look on Mr. Murphy's face was priceless."

"No, it wasn't," Mateo said. "The price was detention. For *all* of us. Right, Zari?" He looked at her meaningfully.

Zari shifted uncomfortably. "Well . . . yeah, I guess."

For a moment, Taylor wore a hard expression, but then she nodded reluctantly. "I get it. Sorry."

Mateo hesitated, then sighed. "Yeah, okay. Can we please get out of here now?"

They headed back down the hallway, looking for an exit.

"Why is everything so quiet?" Mateo asked, glancing around nervously. "Not that I'm complaining or anything."

"The ride's probably shut down," Zari said. "It's closing time."

"That's another reason to hurry," he said.

As if on cue, the lights went out. Emergency lighting glowed softly over doorways, while light from the exterior filtered through the windows, painting the room an eerie green.

"Fantastic," Mateo muttered.

They made their way slowly along the dim hallway and entered the dining room. The disembodied hand stood motionless, still holding the silver dome. Mateo glanced uneasily at the severed head on the platter, which looked even creepier in the gloom.

"The three of us plus your whole family could fit around this table," Zari said to Taylor, who lived with both parents and four siblings. Dinner at Taylor's house was always a fun, noisy event. Zari had no siblings, and since her career-driven parents often worked late, she usually ate alone in front of the TV.

"My family would totally be up for eating here," Taylor said. "Except for Brianna. She scares easier than Mateo." Before he could respond, she pointed to a bright red EMERGENCY EXIT sign high in a corner. "Found it!"

Breathing a sigh of relief, Zari hurried past the table, her dark brown skin glowing red in the light from the exit sign. The wall beneath it was draped with a large tapestry. She pulled it aside, revealing a door. On the crash bar were the words EMERGENCY EXIT ONLY. ALARM WILL SOUND.

"Is this really an emergency?" Taylor asked.

"Are you kidding?" Mateo said. He reached out and pushed the bar.

Nothing happened.

"What the heck?" he said, and tried again, harder this time. "Why won't this open?"

"Stand aside," Taylor said. She strained against the door but with the same results. "It feels like there's something blocking it."

"Who leaves something heavy in front of an emergency door?" Mateo asked. "That's totally a safety code violation."

"Do you really think the high school kids working this ride care about a safety code?" Taylor asked. "But why isn't the alarm going off? We pressed the bar."

Zari pointed up at a sensor. "I think that has to clear the doorframe. Let's try pushing together."

They all pressed against the door, but it wouldn't budge. Whatever was on the other side was too heavy for the three twelve-year-olds. Zari was tall but skinny, and Taylor barely came up to her shoulder. Mateo had a larger build, but he wasn't exactly winning any weightlifting contests.

"Wonderful," he said, slumping to sit on the floor.

"We could go back to the front door," Taylor said. "If we pound and yell, the ride attendant can let us out."

"She's way back at the boathouse across the swamp," Zari said. "I don't think she'd hear us. And we were the last ride of the night, remember? Given the way her face was glued to her phone, I bet she didn't even notice our car came back empty. She's probably halfway home by now."

"But they'll know we're still here when we don't pick up our phones," Taylor said.

Zari shook her head. "A sign over the lockers said unclaimed items would be taken to the lost and found."

Mateo made a frustrated growl. "If they weren't so paranoid about people taking pictures, we'd be able to call for help! This isn't Area 51."

Zari rubbed her temples, trying to think. She always trusted her brain to get her out of tough situations. "No one knows we're at the park. We're supposed to stay overnight at Taylor's house, but her parents are out of town, so no one will miss us."

"Thanks to Taylor," Mateo muttered.

"I didn't hear you complaining when we were having fun all day," she shot back.

They stared at each other in an uneasy silence.

"How about the windows?" Zari said.

Mateo's face brightened. "Yes! Good. We can climb out."

They made their way back to the library. Mateo searched for latches on the large windows overlooking the cemetery, but there were none. "These are all picture windows. They don't open."

Taylor shrugged. "I guess that only leaves one option."

Mateo and Zari watched curiously as Taylor marched over to the fireplace and grabbed a metal poker from the rack of fire tools.

"Might wanna back up," she said.

They scrambled away as Taylor strode over to the window, drew back the poker, and slammed it against the glass. Zari covered her face protectively, waiting to be struck by flying shards.

The poker ricocheted off. Other than a small dent in the center, the window looked unharmed.

"What the . . . ?" Taylor said. She shook out her hand, then struck the window again. The poker bounced off like before. She launched into a furious series of blows, then finally gave up, panting, with a pink flush on her pale cheeks.

"What is *with* this place?" Mateo cried in exasperation.

Zari stepped forward and tapped the glass. It made a muffled plunk. "It's some kind of shatter-resistant plastic. Probably a safety thing." She turned slowly toward her friends, trying to ignore the icy fear raking her gut. "I think we really are trapped in here."

CHAPTER 5

MATEO TURNED away and ran both hands through his hair, leaving it sticking straight up. Taylor gazed at the floor and shuffled her feet.

Zari chewed her lip, racking her brain for something else to try. Having a huge bubble of panic threatening to burst from her stomach didn't help. She blew out a breath. "We have two options: We can either get comfy and wait for the ride to open tomorrow—"

"No way," Mateo said. "I am *not* spending the night in here. Next?"

"We search for another way out," Zari said. "Maybe there's a second emergency exit or something."

Taylor looked up. "I'm good to keep searching, but I'll do whatever. I know this is my fault. I'm really sorry." She looked deflated, like her spark had been snuffed out. While Mateo was relieved she was finally taking some responsibility, even he felt slightly bad for her.

"It's okay," Zari said. "As for searching, I don't know. Some of those beds looked pretty comfortable." She smirked at the stricken look on Mateo's face. "I'm kidding! Let's keep looking."

Sticking close together, they moved through the first floor, trying every door and pulling aside tapestries looking for hidden exits. Most of the doors were fake. One that did work led to an equipment room like they'd seen on the second floor. Inside, they found a charging rack with two flashlights. Mateo snatched one eagerly and flicked it on. It was surprisingly bright, and he clung to it like a security blanket.

Zari offered the other one to Taylor, but she shook her head. "You keep it. I'm good."

After searching the bottom floor with no success, Zari said, "Upstairs?" The others nodded glumly—if they hadn't found a way out on the main floor, what hope did they have going higher?

In the first of the second-floor bedrooms, Mateo tried to ignore the corpse woman who had traumatized him during the ride by sitting up and screaming. Now she lay lifeless and fake-looking.

The friends gazed out a window facing over the swamp and the rest of the park.

"Ride lights are out," Taylor said. "Looks like the park's closed."

"Probably only maintenance and security people left," Zari said.

"And us," said Mateo darkly. He pounded on the window in frustration and yelled for help, but no one was close enough to hear.

They wound their way through each room, testing windows and checking doors. The portraits on the walls were not improving Mateo's mood. One particularly gruesome painting showed a giant eating a headless corpse. Taylor read the small brass plaque on the bottom of the frame. "*Saturn Devouring His Son*. This would look great in my room."

Mateo looked like he'd just sucked a lemon. "How could you sleep with *that* by your bed?"

"You're an artist!" Taylor said. "How can you not appreciate a great painting?"

"I can appreciate the painter's skill," Mateo said, then shuddered. "Just not how they used it."

At the end of a dim hallway, beside a blood-stained suit of armor, they found a staircase spiraling up into darkness. They climbed the narrow steps and emerged into an unfinished attic. Moonlight poured in through circular windows set in the rounded turrets, but most of the space was hidden in deep shadow. Zari shined her flashlight upward, revealing a high ceiling sloped to match the roofline.

Something on one of the rafters caught her eye. "Wow, they put fake bats way up here too," she said. "Maybe this floor is going to be a new part of the ride." Then, with an angry flap of its wings, the bat glared at her, its beady red eyes gleaming in the light.

"Not fake." Mateo gulped. He aimed his flashlight at the ceiling, revealing dozens of bats hanging upside down from the rafters. "I really hate this place."

Zari shivered as the creatures rustled and squeaked. Trying to ignore them, the friends moved slowly around the attic, probing the dark corners with their flashlights.

It was mostly empty. An old dressmaker's dummy stood next to an antique full-length mirror. Stacks of dusty boxes were piled beside discarded tools. Taylor walked over to where a sheet of plywood lay across two sawhorses like a table. Lying on it were huge sheets of paper.

"They're blueprints," she said as the others crowded close.

"Looks like the plans for this ride," Mateo said, flipping through the pages. They were covered with symbols and terms none of them understood, but the outline of Grimstone Manor was clearly visible.

"This should show all the exits, right?" Taylor asked.

"Here's the front door," Zari said, pointing at the main floor page. "And there's the emergency exit we found. But I don't see any others."

"What are these?" asked Mateo, tracing dotted lines with his finger. They were on the main floor but didn't match up with the outline of the building.

Zari chewed her lip, looking thoughtful. "I read that after Hezekiah disappeared, the mansion was abandoned and sat empty for decades until it was finally condemned. The property was eventually bought by the amusement park developers. They restored and expanded the mansion when they turned it into this ride. Maybe those dotted lines show the original foundation."

"So Hezekiah just vanished one day?" Mateo asked.

"Yep," Zari said. "And they never found his body."

They made their way back to the main floor library. Zari and Taylor slumped onto the purple couch, sending up a cloud of dust. While they coughed, Mateo paced near the fireplace.

"I guess we wait till the ride opens in the morning," Zari said once she could speak.

Taylor nodded gloomily, still wrestling with guilt over trapping them in this creepy ride. Feeling restless, she got up to explore the room.

Zari rested her head on the back of the couch and closed her eyes.

"So should we use a bedroom with a rotting corpse?" Taylor asked. "Or stay in the library, where there aren't dead things staring at us?"

"Tough call," Zari murmured.

Taylor eyed the dust trap of a couch as a potential place to sleep. Making a horrendous racket, she dragged a couple of chairs across the floor and placed them near the couch like footstools, just as a muffled thump sounded across the room.

"Sleep here, right, Matty?" Zari asked, her eyes still closed. There was no response. "Matty?" She lifted her head.

Mateo was gone.

CHAPTER 6

ZARI STARED in shock at the fireplace. He'd been right there. She looked quickly around the library.

"Where'd he go?" Taylor asked.

"Mateo?" Zari jumped up from the couch. "Mateo!" She turned to Taylor. "He wouldn't have wandered off somewhere, right?"

"No way," Taylor said. "He wouldn't be caught dead in here alone."

Zari laughed uneasily. She and Taylor ran into the entryway, past the silent butler, and down the hall, calling Mateo's name. After winding their way through the house, they finally came back to the library.

"It's like he vanished!" Taylor said, her voice thick with emotion. "I'm starting to freak out."

Zari fought back a wave of dread as she moved to the fireplace. How could this night get any worse? Feeling faint, she leaned her forehead against the mantel and tried to steady her breathing.

Her spiraling thoughts were interrupted by a faint thumping.

"Mateo? Mateo!" She looked sharply at the fireplace and the book-lined wall in front of her. Taylor ran over and started yelling too.

More thumps.

"Shhh!" Zari said, pressing her ear to the books. "Listen!"

Mateo's muffled voice came from behind the bookcase. "Get me out of here!"

"How?" Zari yelled back.

His voice came again. "Push the ta-too!"

Taylor's face scrunched in confusion. "Do you have a tattoo?"

"I think he said 'statue.'"

"On the mantel!" Mateo shouted. "Push it over!"

Zari looked at the mantel above the fireplace. Sitting on the end near the bookcase was a statue of a crouching werewolf, its lips curled back in a savage snarl. Tentatively, she reached out and pushed it over.

They heard a soft click, and the bookcase beside the fireplace swung back, revealing a yawning black opening.

A figure hurtled out of the darkness.

"Mateo!" Taylor cried, and threw her arms around him as the bookcase clicked shut.

"How'd you get back there?" Zari asked.

"I was leaning against those bookshelves next to the fireplace," Mateo said, his voice shaking.

"That werewolf statue was creeping me out, so I pushed it over. Then the bookcase swung in, and I fell through. I tried to yell but sucked in some spit and started choking. Then the bookcase shut and locked me out."

Zari looked over at the mantel. The werewolf statue was standing again. She pushed it over, and the trick bookcase opened.

"Catch it!" she said. Taylor grabbed the bookcase before it swung shut. Zari examined the bottom of the statue. A wire connected to its base ran through a hole in the top of the mantel and disappeared.

Taylor peered into the secret doorway. "Is this some part of the ride that we missed?"

"I don't think so," Mateo said. "There's no track for the cars."

They shined their flashlights through the opening. A gray stone stairway descended into the darkness.

"I wonder what's down there," Zari said. "And why is it hidden behind a bookcase?"

"Maybe it's like *The Phantom of the Opera*!" Taylor said. "The Phantom made all kinds of secret doors so he could sneak around the opera house without being seen."

Mateo crinkled his nose. "He sounds like a creep."

"Let's check it out," Taylor said.

"Go *down* there?" said Mateo. "I just got out!"

"She's got a point," Zari said. "It's the only place we haven't searched. There might be an exit."

"We're on the ground floor, and these steps go down," Mateo said. "How could they possibly lead to an exit?"

Zari shrugged. "My grandparents have stairs in their cellar that lead up to the outside. Maybe this place has something like that. We can at least look."

"Why are all of our options really bad?" Mateo muttered.

Zari took a sharp piece of wood from the fire-box and wedged it under the secret door to prop it open. Since Taylor was eager to explore, Zari gave her the flashlight, and they gazed at the narrow stone staircase.

"Did you go down these steps?" Zari asked Mateo.

"No, I pretty much just clung to the trick wall and wailed for help."

They descended into the gloom. At the bottom of the steps was a wide passageway of rough stone running left and right. A stale, musty odor hung in the air. The ceiling arched overhead, and the darkness pressed close. In the wall opposite the steps was an alcove filled with partially melted candles. Above it hung a smooth stone slab with a message engraved in formal lettering:

"I don't know what that means, but I don't like it," said Mateo.

"It's French," Zari said.

"Can you read it?" Taylor asked. Zari studied French in school and had been to France several times to visit her aunt.

"Um . . . *ici* means 'here,'" Zari said, her face scrunched in concentration. "And *nous* is 'we.' I'm not sure what the third word is."

"Looks kinda like *celebrar*," Mateo said. "That means 'celebrate' in Spanish."

"Could be," Zari said. "Spanish and French have a lot of similar words."

"What about *la morte*?" Taylor asked.

Zari looked uncomfortable. "It means . . . 'death.'"

"Here we celebrate *death*?" Mateo exclaimed. "Why would that be carved below an amusement park ride?"

"I don't think this has anything to do with the ride," Taylor said. "It looks like a creepy old basement or something."

Zari twisted a hair coil around her finger. "What if this *is* an old basement?"

"But what kind of person would celebrate death in their basement?" Mateo asked, then his face fell. "Oh. You mean . . ."

They all spoke together: "Hezekiah Crawly."

CHAPTER 7

"TERRIFIC," MATEO groaned. "What's worse than being trapped overnight in a fake haunted house? Exploring a *real* haunted basement."

"Would you rather crawl into bed with Screamy Corpse Lady?" Taylor asked.

"Possibly," Mateo said, eyeing the dark passage uneasily. "Where's the light switch?"

"I don't think there's electricity down here," Zari said, examining the alcove. Near the candles lay a rectangular brass container about the size of a pack of playing cards. Flipping open the tarnished top, she found rough-hewn matches. She struck one against the wall, then lit the candles.

Grasping the loop of a candle holder, Zari followed Taylor and Mateo as they led the way along the passage with their flashlights. The flickering flame cast eerie shadows, and their shuffling feet seemed unnaturally loud in the deep silence.

"Basements are usually big, open spaces," Mateo said. "What's with this hallway?"

"There's definitely not a rec room down here," Taylor said.

They reached a corner in the passage. A second, smaller corridor branched off at an angle. Staying in the larger passageway, Taylor stepped confidently around the corner. The floor of the passage now sloped steadily downward. Mateo and Zari followed cautiously and found her intently examining the wall.

"It's all bumpy," Taylor said. "This doesn't look like stone."

Where the rough stone ended were rows of uneven, knoblike shapes, off-white and each about the size of a large egg. Something about them seemed familiar to Zari, but she couldn't place it. As she brushed her fingertips against them, Mateo gasped and stumbled back.

"What?" Taylor asked.

He pointed a trembling finger at the wall. "B-bones."

Zari stared at the wall in confusion. Then it clicked. The roughly circular shapes were the ends of human bones, stacked on top of each other. Hundreds of them. With a sharp breath, she snatched her hand away and wiped it on her shirt.

"Would someone please tell me why the walls are made of *bones*?" Mateo asked.

"I've seen something like this before," Zari said. "When I visited my aunt last summer in Paris, she took us to a famous crypt under the city. A long time ago, they moved bones from overcrowded cemeteries down there. It's a tourist attraction now."

"So you're saying . . . ?" Mateo began.

"This isn't a basement," Zari said, feeling goose bumps rise on her arms that had nothing to do with the chill air. "It's a crypt!"

"That would make sense of the sign back there," Taylor said. "*Here we celebrate death.*"

Mateo's face looked ghostly in the candlelight. "And I didn't think things could get any worse."

"Oh, come on," Taylor said. "Dead stuff can't hurt you."

"Said the victim in every horror movie ever," Mateo replied.

They continued along the downward-sloping passage. Zari kept lighting candles whenever she found them. They soon came to a thick, bulging column in the center of the passageway.

"Please tell me those aren't what I think they are," Mateo said, staring wide-eyed at the column.

"Okay, they're not human skulls," Taylor said. "Just kidding, they totally are."

The skulls were arranged in diamond patterns, each one circled by a fringe of finger bones. Arm bones formed zigzagging bands along the top and bottom of the column. Zari thought it would have been pretty if it wasn't so morbid.

"Hezekiah's interior decorator must have done Dracula's castle," Mateo said.

On the far side of the column, the larger sloping passageway continued, while a smaller, level corridor ran off at a right angle into the darkness. "It's like a maze down here," Zari said.

Mateo looked ill. "By my math, human skulls plus possibly getting lost equals time to go back to the library."

Taylor's jaw dropped. "Are you kidding? This is the coolest place ever!"

"I want to keep searching for a way out," Zari said firmly.

"It'll go faster if we split up," Taylor said.

Mateo's eyes almost popped from his skull. "Not. Happening. We stick *together*."

"You're probably right," Taylor said. "Monsters like to pick off kids when they're alone. Let's try this new corridor."

Taylor had led them partway down the smaller corridor when she froze, nearly causing Mateo to bump into her.

"A little warning next—" he began, then stopped.

Puzzled, Zari looked over Mateo's shoulder and bit back a cry.

Taylor's flashlight illuminated a spot where the wall met the floor. Standing in the glow was a pair of legs.

And they weren't human.

CHAPTER 8

THE LEGS were covered in sleek black fur. The heels were raised, like the creature was balancing on the balls of its feet. Strong, curved claws extended from each toe.

It stood without moving. The light in Taylor's hand trembled as she slowly raised the beam. Huge clawed hands hung beside muscular thighs. The light revealed a massive chest, a thick, forward-curving neck, and finally, the head. A long, open muzzle thrust out, filled with wicked-looking fangs. Large triangular ears perched above piercing eyes.

It was a huge werewolf.

They all stood without breathing.

Taylor leaped forward and punched the monster in the stomach. Then she started laughing and shook her hand as if it was bruised. "It's a statue!" she said, rapping her knuckles against the monster's chest. "I really had you two!"

Mateo made an exasperated sound as Zari glared at Taylor. "You knew the whole time?"

"Not at first," she admitted with a shrug. "But I figured it out."

"And thought it would be fun to give me a heart attack?" Mateo asked.

"Well . . . yeah," Taylor replied sheepishly.

The werewolf towered above them, its head almost brushing the top of the alcove where it stood. The entire monster looked carved from a single piece of black marble. A large blue gemstone hung around the statue's neck from a thin gold chain.

"Look at the detail on this thing," Zari said, holding her candle up to the creature's face. "I never knew stone could be so lifelike."

"The mantel statue was bad enough," Mateo said. "I'm not going to sleep for a week after seeing this."

"I'd love it for my room," Taylor said longingly.

Mateo shook his head. "I do not understand your brain."

They continued past the werewolf, and soon the corridor ended in an arched doorway. After stepping through, Zari used her candle to light an old-fashioned torch in a nearby wall bracket, and they squinted at the sudden brightness.

Even with all the frightening things they'd seen already, Taylor gasped. "Whoa! I think we found the rec room."

They stood on the edge of a large circular chamber with a domed ceiling covered in strange symbols. Seven more archways were evenly spaced around the chamber, marking the entrances to other dark corridors. There were small alcoves in the walls between the archways, but instead of candles, each one contained a winged gargoyle with its contorted face peering out. Eight waist-high stone slabs were arranged in a ring along the walls. On top of each slab lay a body, tightly wrapped in wide strips of cream-colored cloth.

"Mummies," Mateo said, his voice sounding higher than usual. "Why are there mummies?"

"Well, this *is* a crypt," Taylor said. "Are they Hezekiah's family or something?"

"Could be," Zari said. "Or maybe he really did rob graves." She stared mutely at the bodies, chewing her lip. "I wonder why these are lying out in the open? A mummy is usually in a sarcophagus."

"A sarcopha-what-sis?" Taylor asked.

"The case a mummy goes in," Zari said. "Like King Tut."

She took the flaming torch from its bracket and used it to light three others, fully illuminating the chamber.

"It's like this room is the hub of a wheel," Taylor said, "and all these passageways are the spokes."

"Check out the floor," Mateo said.

An intricate spiderweb design covered a large circular area in the center of the room. Where the lines of the pattern connected were small holes about an inch wide. There were dozens of them. In the center of the web was a stone statue about three feet high, carved in the shape of a bloated spider. Two of its long legs stretched toward the ceiling and held a bowl full of something that glimmered in the torchlight.

"And I thought live spiders were bad," Mateo said.

"Forget the spider," Taylor said, approaching the bowl and reaching out her hand. "We've got gold coins!"

"Wait!" Zari cried.

"What?" Taylor asked. "Hezekiah's long gone. It's not like stealing or anything. Is it?"

"It's not that," Zari said. "But a bowl full of gold coins just sitting out in a crypt? It could be a trap."

Taylor hesitated, then pulled her hand back and joined Zari as she examined one of the mummies. Mateo stood as far away as possible.

"There's another one of those blue gems," Zari said, pointing to a brooch pinned to the wrappings on the mummy's chest. "Same stone as the werewolf necklace."

Taylor went to the next mummy. "This guy has one too. They all do."

The friends left the mummy room through an archway on the opposite side of the chamber. They soon came to a large alcove with a life-sized statue of a reptile woman, tall and heavily muscled, with a thick tail that reached the ground. Her hands ended in three wide fingers, each tipped with a sharp, curved claw. The monster's eyes bulged over a squarish mouth filled with blunt fangs. Small tentacle-like feelers stood out from her face. The stone was dark green and covered with intricately carved scales. Like the werewolf, a blue gem hung around her neck from a narrow gold chain.

"Do you want this for your room, too?" Mateo asked Taylor.

"I don't think so," she said, wrinkling her nose at the creature. "Something about this one even creeps *me* out."

"So why all the statues and elaborate decorations?" Zari asked. "What's the point? It seems pretty over-the-top for a crypt."

They continued past the lizard woman statue, and soon the corridor ended at another skull column, identical to the first. A wide passageway sloped up to the right and down to the left. Zari raised her candle and gazed in both directions. "So should we go back up toward the stairs or further down?"

Her friends answered simultaneously.

"Down," said Taylor.

"Up," said Mateo.

Zari gave them a grim smile, then turned left, heading deeper into the crypt. The passage continued sloping down, finally ending at the largest archway they'd seen so far.

They stepped through the opening, and Zari lit wall torches on either side.

For a moment, none of them spoke.

Finally, Taylor gave a low whistle. "Speaking of over-the-top . . ."

CHAPTER 9

TAYLOR'S VOICE echoed through a vast rectangular hall that stretched the full width of the crypt. The gray walls were decorated with more bones than she could count. Embedded in the stone were human rib cages arranged in sweeping arcs over rows of crossed femurs. Skulls were laid out in large swirling patterns. Like the mummy chamber, the ceiling was covered in strange symbols. Three towering black pillars stood along the opposite wall.

Down the face of each was a single word spelled out in human bones. Together, it read:

VOICI LE MAÎTRE

Taylor gazed around her in awe. *What is this place?* she wondered.

Below the central pillar stood a tall platform. In the middle of the platform rested a large grayish-white coffin. A mysterious blue glow came from an object on a nearby pedestal.

Standing on the intricately tiled floor of the chamber were five human skeletons. Zari could tell they weren't like the plastic one in her middle school's science room. These skeletons wore golden helmets over their skulls and held short swords with wide blades. They stood at attention in a protective arc in front of the coffin platform.

"Does anyone else feel like we shouldn't be here?" Mateo whispered.

Zari nodded, unable to speak. Taylor was the first to break the spell. She walked slowly toward the platform, and Zari followed, dragging a reluctant Mateo by his elbow. They had entered from one corner of the chamber, and Zari noticed two more archways in the same wall, entrances to corridors that led back toward the mummy room.

They reached the nearest skeleton. Its empty eye sockets stared vacantly at nothing. A familiar blue gem decorated the front of its helmet.

"I . . . I think they're real," Zari said.

"But how do you get real skeletons to stay together like this?" Taylor asked, gently touching its hand. "*And* hold a sword. I don't see any wires."

Moving between the unnerving skeletons, they approached the platform. Wide steps ran along the front edge with huge urns standing at either end. On each urn was a picture of a strange creature with a beaklike muzzle and glowing green eyes that looked like a demonic chimpanzee.

"Check out the freaky monster painted on this vase," said Mateo, wrinkling his nose.

"It's an urn," Zari said.

"That monster's called an urn?"

"Not the monster. The vase."

"What?"

"The vase is an urn."

"But you just called it a vase."

"Yeah, but that type of vase—"

Taylor gave an exasperated sigh. "Zari, make like *Frozen* and let it go."

They moved to climb the platform steps. As Mateo glanced back nervously at the line of silent skeletons, he tripped on a raised tile and fell to the floor. *Smooth, Mateo,* he thought. His face flushed red. He was about to push himself to his feet when he noticed something shiny under the lip of each step, glinting dully in his flashlight beam. *Is that glass?*

"Stop!" he shouted.

Taylor's foot hovered over the first step as she stared at him quizzically.

Mateo crawled forward and examined the underside of each step. Taylor and Zari knelt beside him. Wedged into where the tread rested on the riser were small vials of glass filled with a swirling blue substance.

"I think if you put weight on these steps, the glass would break and release whatever's inside," Mateo said.

Zari bit her lip. "With the way it's hidden, it must be some kind of trap."

"What's so scary about a little blue stuff?" Taylor asked.

Zari glanced uneasily at the chamber's bone decorations. "Let's not find out."

She lit several torches mounted nearby, then took one to replace her candle. Avoiding the steps, they clambered onto the platform and made their way slowly toward the coffin. It was unusually large, made of polished white marble streaked with gray veins. Engraved on the lid was a name.

Hezekiah Crawly.

Zari sucked in a sharp breath.

Mateo's eyes widened. "I guess we know where Hezekiah Crawly disappeared to."

"Can you translate those words?" Taylor asked, gesturing toward the pillars.

Zari looked up at the message, VOICI LE MAÎTRE, gruesomely spelled out in human bones. "*Le* is 'the.' *Voici* is like 'here' or 'behold.' And the last word . . . I'm guessing 'master'? So I think it says 'Behold the master.'"

Mateo snorted in disgust. "Sounds on-brand for Hezekiah."

Their eyes moved to an ornate, waist-high pedestal that stood beside the coffin. On its flat marble top sat a life-sized human skull made of clear glass. A bright blue mist swirled and danced inside the skull, curling back on itself like a living thing.

Taylor sucked in a breath. "It's *beautiful*." She reached out her hand to touch it.

Mateo grabbed her arm. "Don't."

She looked at him in surprise. "What are you doing?"

"Don't touch it," he said. "We don't know what it is."

Taylor pulled her arm from his grip and grumbled, "That's what I'm trying to figure out."

He stepped between her and the skull. Zari was surprised. Normally when Taylor got fired up, Mateo backed down. "That thing is bad," he said.

"And how do you know that?" Taylor asked scornfully.

"Do I need to point out where we're standing?" he said, gesturing at the creepy chamber. "And that blue mist looks the same as what's under the steps. Besides . . . I just know."

"Oh, so the guy who's never been to a haunted house before is suddenly an expert on spooky stuff?" Taylor said.

"Yeah . . . I mean, no, but . . . you can't touch it," Mateo said firmly.

"Excuse me?" she said, her eyes blazing. "I can *do* what I *want*."

"Not this time," he said crossing his arms stubbornly. "I'm not letting you make things even *worse*."

"Get out of my *way*," Taylor growled, but Mateo shook his head.

"Stop arguing," Zari pleaded, but Taylor launched herself forward, trying to reach past Mateo for the skull. He grabbed her wrist, and she shoved him. When Mateo stepped back to catch his balance, Taylor wrenched her arm away. Her flailing hand accidentally struck the skull, sending it spinning across its slick marble perch.

They froze, their eyes locked on the glass skull as it balanced precariously on the edge of the pedestal.

"No!" Mateo cried, and lurched to catch it.

He was too late. The skull slipped over the edge. It struck the tile floor and shattered into a thousand pieces.

For a few moments, they all gazed at the glass shards in disbelief. Then Mateo rounded on Taylor. "Way to go! Are you happy now?"

Taylor's eyes crackled with fire. "Don't you *dare* blame that on me! That was *your* fault, you controlling little twerp!"

"*Someone* has to control you," he said, his face flushed. "You certainly can't control yourself!"

"Control myself?" Taylor shouted. "Oh, that's hilarious coming from you. You do enough controlling for all of us!"

Mateo inflated like a blowfish. "I am *sick* and *tired* of cleaning up your—"

"Will you both shut up!" Zari yelled at the top of her lungs.

Taylor and Mateo looked at her in surprise, their argument momentarily forgotten.

"I can't *stand* you two fighting anymore!" Zari said. "Taylor, I love you, but would you *please* stop being so reckless? We're really sick of it." The smug grin that blossomed on Mateo's face quickly faded when she wheeled toward him. "And *you*. Caution is a good thing, but you take it *way* too far. You really suck the fun out of everything."

Zari paused, breathing heavily, and stared at their shocked faces. She was pretty shocked herself. She'd never spoken to anyone like that before, let alone her best friends.

Taylor glared at Zari with her jaw clenched and her hands balled into fists. But then her expression softened slightly and her fists relaxed. "Okay, Zar. I hear you."

Mateo shuffled his feet, looking like a whipped puppy. "Um . . . You're right. Sorry."

They stood in awkward silence, not looking at each other. After a few moments, Zari said, "I'm sorry, too. I haven't spoken up when I should have. I'll do better."

"Can you do it without the yelling next time?" Taylor asked, the corners of her lips curling upward.

"Deal," Zari said with a faint smile. She looked at Mateo. "Are we okay?"

Instead of replying, he stared past her with a confused expression, then pointed.

The blue mist, now freed from the glass skull, had formed a thick ribbon that slithered into the air like a cobra rising from a snake charmer's basket. They watched in amazement as the writhing mist split in two. One strand slid smoothly under the lid of the coffin, while the other moved slowly across the stage and down the steps. It reached the first skeleton and paused at the front of its helmet. Then the mist moved down the row, touching each skeleton's helmet before turning and disappearing through an archway in the opposite wall.

Finally, Taylor said, "That was weird."

"Should we be worried?" Zari asked.

"Probably," said Mateo.

They stood in tense silence, waiting for something to happen. After twenty long, uneventful seconds, Zari sighed in relief. She hadn't realized she'd been holding her breath. Taylor grinned sheepishly, and even Mateo cracked a smile. The harmless blue smoke show was over.

Then the skeletons began to move.

CHAPTER 10

THE FRIENDS gasped as the five skeletons standing on the floor below the platform began to twitch. At first, their movements were slow and jerky, like stiff marionettes being controlled by strings. Then they began moving more freely, as if awakening from a long sleep. Mateo's brain screamed at him to run, but his feet felt like they'd sunk into the platform.

One of the skulls rotated slowly toward them. Its empty eye sockets were pools of shadow in the flickering torchlight. The skeleton took a step.

Mateo whimpered. "I'm ready to wake up now."

"Run!" Taylor yelled. She grabbed her friends' arms and pulled them toward the front of the platform. Zari stumbled along, her mind reeling in horror. As they pounded down the steps, they heard the crunch of breaking glass. Blue mist swirled around their feet as the hidden vials shattered. They reached the chamber floor and flew through the row of bony guardians.

The nearest exit was centered on the far wall of the chamber. They raced toward it, followed by a strange clacking sound. The five skeletons were now fully awake. The bones of their feet clattered against the tile floor as they rushed after the fleeing group, with swords raised. Formerly dark and cold, the blue gems on the skeletons' helmets now glowed with an inner fire.

The friends hurtled through the archway and up a new sloping corridor. Behind them, the skeletons' footsteps grew louder.

They saw flickering torchlight ahead, and moments later, they burst into the mummy room. Mateo's heart felt like it backflipped. The blue mist hovered over each body. A hand twitched. Then the leg of another. The mummies were stirring.

"This way!" Taylor raced past the spider statue toward the candlelit corridor they'd used earlier.

She and Zari had almost reached the archway when Mateo wailed, "Wait! Don't leave me!" One of the mummies had grasped the back of his shirt as he ran past. The fabric pulled tight across Mateo's chest as he strained to break free. His face was a mask of terror, his eyes huge and pleading for help.

The mummy rose slowly to a seated position on its stone bed. The blue gem pinned to its chest glowed brightly. The monster reached for Mateo with its other hand.

Swallowing her fear, Zari ran back, grabbed Mateo's outstretched arm, and pulled. For a moment, they were trapped in a horrible tug-of-war. Then with a sharp tearing sound, a piece of Mateo's shirt ripped off in the mummy's hand, and he was free.

They followed Taylor out of the chamber. As they raced along the familiar corridor, Zari glanced at the tall alcove in the wall.

The werewolf statue was gone.

"Aw, duckweed!" Taylor spat.

Trying not to think of what the missing werewolf meant, they kept running. They turned at the skull column and continued up the sloping corridor, retracing their steps. The stairs were close now. They were almost out. As they rounded the final corner, the clacking of skeleton feet drew nearer.

"There it is!" Taylor cried.

They turned into the stairwell and pounded up the stone steps to the manor. They would still be locked in the ride, but at least they'd be free from this horror show.

Taylor froze. Zari rammed into her, knocking her smaller friend to the steps.

"Why'd you stop?" Zari cried.

Then she noticed a gamey, musky odor. A deep growl came from the shadows above them. Trembling, she raised her torch higher. In front of the door, wearing a glowing blue necklace, stood the werewolf. Behind him, the bookcase was shut tight.

They were trapped.

CHAPTER 11

MATEO SCREAMED as the now-very-much-alive werewolf reached for Zari, his wicked-looking claws outstretched. Her own cry of terror lodged in her throat. She dropped and reflexively curled into a ball, which caused her to start rolling down the stairs.

A howl of rage and pain echoed wildly in the stone stairwell. Zari stuck out her legs to stop herself and looked back up the steps. A piece of wood protruded from the werewolf's thigh.

Taylor whirled around. "Go! Go!"

She pulled Zari to her feet, and they flew down the stairs, then tumbled into the passageway. The skeletons surged forward, their swords raised. Taylor pushed Mateo out of the way as one swung its weapon. The blade struck the stone wall with a clang. A second skeleton closed in on Mateo as he lay on the floor.

"No!" Zari stretched out her arm, but she was too far away to stop it.

The werewolf hurtled out of the stairwell. In his eagerness to get to them, he crashed carelessly into the approaching skeleton as it swept its weapon down. The strike missed Mateo as the werewolf's momentum drove the bony warrior into the wall. The helmet flew from its skull and came to rest at Taylor's feet, the blue gem dimming. The skeleton collapsed in a clatter of bones and lay still.

The werewolf faced them with a menacing snarl. Zari scrambled backward, but knew they couldn't escape in time. Before the monster could pounce, the remaining skeletons attacked him. The werewolf howled and spun around, revealing a gash across his back.

While the werewolf fended off the skeletons, the three friends raced around a corner and plunged down a new corridor leading back toward the mummy room. When Taylor spotted a door in the wall, she threw it open and darted inside. Mateo and Zari followed her, then quickly closed the door.

"Lock it!" Taylor said.

Zari scanned the handle. "It doesn't lock!"

Mateo grabbed a wooden chair and jammed it under the knob. They stood panting and listening for sounds of pursuit.

They were in a large room filled with shelves and tables holding an odd assortment of items. Taylor looked around frantically, then hurried to a tall storage cabinet in a dark corner. She opened it and whispered, "Help me!"

Zari shoved her torch into an empty wall bracket, then helped the others quickly remove dusty boxes, empty glass jars, and a leatherbound journal from the cabinet. They climbed inside and closed the doors.

Crammed together, they tried to quiet their heavy breathing. Faint glimmers of torchlight filtered in through the cracks around the doors. They listened intently for something trying to enter the room, but for the moment, all was still. In stunned silence, they each tried to process the bizarre nightmare they'd wandered into.

"This isn't possible," Mateo said softly. "None of those things are supposed to be *real*."

"Somebody forgot to tell the monsters," Taylor said.

"What happened with the werewolf on the stairs?" Zari asked. "I thought we were dog food."

"The piece of wood you used to prop open the door was lying on the steps," Taylor said. "It had a sharp end, so I stabbed the werewolf in the leg."

Zari's jaw dropped in amazement. "And saved my life. Thank you."

"Why did the werewolf and the skeletons fight each other?" Mateo asked.

"Wolfy was chasing us, and that skeleton got in his way," Taylor said. "I guess the skeletons didn't like him taking out one of their own."

"So now what?" Mateo asked. "Even if we could make it back to the steps, the bookcase is shut. Without someone to open it from the other side, we can't get through!"

"We'll have to find another way," Taylor said.

"Just like that, huh?" Mateo said. "Overconfident much? Oh wait, you are." He lowered his head and took a deep breath, trying to slow his rampaging heart. He was more frightened than he'd ever been in his life, and he couldn't see a way out. Still, he knew that giving up and sniping at Taylor wouldn't solve anything. "I'm sorry. I'm just really freaked out."

"I get it. We're good," Taylor said. "There are still some corridors we haven't used yet. Maybe one of them has an exit."

Zari chewed her lip. "And we never finished searching the coffin chamber."

"You want to go all the way back *there*?" Mateo asked. "We could get lost!"

"I don't think so," Taylor said, a look of concentration on her face as she pictured the crypt layout in her mind. "The wider passageways make a big rectangle that slopes up to the stairs at one end and down to the coffin chamber at the other. The mummy room is in the middle, and the smaller corridors spread out from it like a spiderweb. Everything's connected."

Zari nodded. "We can search the corridors we haven't tried yet on our way down to the coffin chamber. But we'll need something to fight with."

"Fight?" said Mateo in alarm.

"These monsters don't exactly seem interested in conversation," Taylor said.

"The skeletons have swords," Zari said. "But it would be hard to get those."

They were quiet for a moment, then Mateo said in a quavering voice, "This room has a lot of stuff on the tables. Maybe we can find something useful."

Taylor cracked open the cabinet door and peered around the room. "All clear," she whispered, and they quietly climbed out. Zari retrieved her torch from the wall and lit two more.

One table was covered with dried plants, clay pots, and bowls with stone grinders. On another, wicked-looking knives, sharp metal hooks with wooden handles, and other tools none of them recognized lay in neat rows. Elsewhere, a handful of blue gemstones were scattered beside what looked like jewelers' tools. Clear containers filled with different-colored liquids were neatly arranged on shelves, along with a small wooden rack holding a row of glass vials plugged with rubber tops. Blue mist swirled sluggishly inside most of the vials, while a few contained a mist of sickly green. Pairs of thick shackles were secured to one of the stone walls by heavy chains.

"This place looks like a twisted science lab mixed with a demented jewelry shop," Mateo said.

Taylor held up a roll of cream-colored fabric bandages. "I think the mummies were wrapped here."

"That would explain these tools," Zari said. "They're for prepping the bodies."

"What do you mean, 'prepping the bodies'?" Mateo asked, then his face fell. "Why do I immediately regret asking that question?"

"Remember world history with Ms. Kumar last year?" Zari said. "Ancient Egyptians would remove a dead person's organs and stuff the body with preservatives before wrapping it up."

"And they put the guts in clay jars," Mateo said, shrinking away from a row of covered pottery on a table.

Zari spotted a huge book resting on a stand. Its black leather cover was cracked and worn, and the silver metal binding was tarnished.

"This is wild," she said, flipping slowly through the stiff pages. Colorful artwork surrounded handwritten text, laid out like poetry in a language she didn't recognize.

"Those pictures are gruesome," Mateo said. "I'm guessing these aren't nursery rhymes."

Zari checked the cover. "*Liber de Morte*," she murmured, chewing her lower lip. "I think this is a book of dark magic. Probably filled with nasty spells."

"That rhyme is sounding more accurate all the time," Taylor said. "Hezekiah really *was* into dark magic."

Zari nodded slowly. "I think this was his necromancy lab. Where he tried to raise an undead army."

"An army of mummies, skeletons, and werewolves," Mateo said.

"All the more reason to get out of here," Taylor said. "Pick a weapon."

Mateo followed her to the table holding the knives. Zari stood motionless before the book, with a slightly glazed expression.

"Zar, are you coming?" Taylor asked.

Zari ignored her and murmured, "There's something missing."

"Missing?" said Mateo. "What's missing?"

Zari didn't answer but gazed intently around the room. After a few moments, her eyes fell on the journal they'd pulled from the storage cabinet. "Of course," she said, rushing toward it.

Mateo glanced at Taylor. "Do you know what she's talking about?"

Taylor rolled her eyes. "Do I ever?"

Zari grabbed the journal and began paging through it. "Yes! This is it."

"You're doing it again," Taylor grumbled. "Speak. Not all of us have your Google brain."

"What?" Zari said, looking up at them. "Oh, sorry! Notes. That's what was missing. In a lab, there's always a place where the scientist records the results of their experiments. If this was Hezekiah's necromancy lab, I figured there should be notes. And I found them!" She waved the journal excitedly.

"And his old notes are important because . . . ?" Mateo asked.

"Besides being super interesting, we might learn something helpful about the monsters," Zari said. "Never hurts to know your enemy."

She opened the journal on the table as Mateo and Taylor approached. "Listen to this: *The magic is mine; it came to me. I am no longer just a man. I have the right, the duty, to rule. But the others will not see it—the sheep never honor the wolf. So I must take what is mine, and to do that, I need an army unlike any the world has ever seen.*"

"So we were right," Taylor said, sounding uncharacteristically subdued.

Zari continued flipping pages. "He's got notes on each of the monsters. Looks like he started with the mummies. In this entry, he's all excited that he raised them from the dead, but later writes that they're too slow and clumsy."

"Sounds like you, Mateo," said Taylor.

He reached over and tugged her ponytail.

"Urgh, you know I hate that!" she said.

"Don't make fun of me, then. What else, Zari?"

"Skeletons were next. He writes that they're faster and better fighters, but calls them fragile."

"They don't seem fragile to me," Taylor said.

Zari scanned more pages. Many of the entries were filled with formulas or illegible scrawl, or were written in a language she didn't understand. "Here's something: *The werewolf is almost unfazed by injury, and his strength is astonishing—I was forced to install heavier chains to restrain him. But he is wild and difficult to control, having retained little of his former humanity. The Medusa Spell, which immobilizes*

him in a stonelike state, is the only thing that can con-
tain him for long. I believe he hates me for what I've
done to him and would kill me if he had the chance."

"Can't say I blame Wolfy," Taylor said.

"I almost feel sorry for him," said Mateo. "Almost. I mean, he's still terrifying."

The sound of footsteps moving through the passageways drifted through the door.

"We should get moving," Taylor said. "They'll find us if we stay in one place too long. Grab a weapon."

Mateo and Zari both selected long knives while Taylor chose a large hooked blade with a wooden handle. They headed for the door. On a whim, Zari grabbed a stone pestle from where it sat in a mortar.

"What's that?" Taylor asked. "It looks like the world's smallest club."

"It's for crushing plants and spices," Zari said. "It might be useful."

"If we run into any possessed flowers, you can grind them to death," Mateo said as Zari stuffed the pestle into her pocket.

Taylor quietly removed the chair from under the door handle, then paused to listen. "Leave the flashlights off unless we need them. The candles and torches we lit should give us enough light."

"If we run into anything, we try a different passage," Zari said. "Fighting is our last resort."

"And we *stick together*," Mateo said, the fear evident in his voice. "No matter what."

Taylor nodded. "No matter what."

CHAPTER 12

AFTER MAKING sure there were no creatures lurking nearby, they slipped into the dark corridor. To the left, they could see the distant torchlight of the mummy chamber. Taylor led them in the opposite direction, back to the wide passageway, then around a corner heading toward the coffin chamber. Down the sloping passage ahead of them, candles flickered, casting grim shadows on one of the skull columns.

When they drew close to the column, Taylor stopped to check the passageway ahead for movement. As Zari shifted to look past Mateo, her shoulder bumped into the wall. Except it didn't feel like stone. It was softer.

A hand dropped heavily on her shoulder. A hand wrapped in thick bandages. She shrieked and tried to jerk away, but its grip was too strong. The movement revealed a blue gem glowing softly in the darkness. Mateo froze, gaping up at the mummy, his knife trembling in his hand.

Taylor pushed past him and swung her hooked blade at the mummy's outstretched arm. The sharp metal sliced completely through the withered wrist. With a wavering groan, the mummy pulled back its dry stump, leaving the severed hand still clinging to Zari's shoulder.

"Urgh, gross!" Zari cried. She plucked it off and threw it to the ground.

As they rushed forward into the candlelight, a skeleton jumped out from behind the skull column with its sword raised.

"Duck!" Zari yelled, then dove to the ground, followed by Mateo. The skeleton swept the weapon in a wide arc, clipping Taylor's ponytail as she threw herself to the floor.

The skeleton stepped toward her and lifted its sword for another strike. Taylor kicked out and caught the bony warrior in the back of the knee. Its leg buckled, and the skeleton collapsed. Scrambling to her feet, she snarled, "*Nobody* touches my ponytail."

They bolted around the skull column and down the sloping passageway toward Hezekiah's chamber.

When they reached the end of the passage, they cautiously peered around the corner into the vast coffin room. The torches Zari had lit earlier shone brightly. Standing near the doorway, as if they'd been waiting for the trio, were a pair of mummies. With a wail, the monsters lurched forward, arms outstretched.

"Go back!" cried Mateo.

They retreated up the passage with Mateo in the lead. The blue gems on the mummies' chests glowed as they shuffled after them.

Mateo clicked on his flashlight, then came to an abrupt halt. Zari and Taylor slid to a stop behind him.

The skeleton raced toward them down the passageway.

They were trapped.

"What do we do?" asked Mateo with an edge of hysteria in his voice.

"Fight!" Taylor yelled. Brandishing her hooked blade, she leaped past him to take on the skeleton.

Trying to draw courage from Taylor, Zari held out her knife toward the advancing mummies. Mateo's panicked breathing accelerated, and soon he began hyperventilating. With his back against the rough wall, he slid slowly to the ground between his friends.

The air filled with the clank of metal on metal from Taylor's duel with the skeleton. The nearest mummy stepped into the wavering beam of Mateo's flashlight. The wrapping around its face had separated, revealing dead-looking eyes. Its mouth parted in a groan as it reached for Zari.

With a cry of fear and rage, she lunged under the mummy's outstretched arm and slashed her knife across its belly. Dried spices tumbled from the gash. Then she remembered its guts were in a clay pot in the necromancy lab. A sickly fragrant odor filled the passage, and she gagged. "You smell like my grandma's Poo-Pourri bathroom spray!"

Completely unfazed, the mummy reached down and grabbed Zari's arm in a shockingly strong grip. She tried to break free, but the mummy dragged her relentlessly toward it.

Then with a strangled cry, Mateo leaped forward. He slashed awkwardly with his knife, striking the mummy across the face. The bandages split and fell away, revealing a skull-like head tightly covered with blackened skin. Its bloodless lips were pulled back in a revolting grin.

The second mummy lurched toward them and bumped clumsily into the first. The mummy holding Zari was knocked off-balance and cracked its head against the wall. Oblivious to the blow, it kept pulling Zari closer. Mateo turned to face the newcomer, leaving Zari to struggle alone.

The mummy wrapped its other arm around Zari's shoulder and pressed her to its chest. The coarse wrappings scratched her face, and she sucked in whiffs of moldy incense. She wriggled wildly in terror, but the mummy squeezed her tighter, forcing the air from her lungs.

With her arms pinned, Zari couldn't use her knife. As ineffective as her first strike had been, it was the only weapon she had. Spots danced before her eyes as she struggled to breathe. One blue spot refused to move, remaining steady beside her trapped hand—the glowing gem pinned to the mummy's chest.

The gem. It had begun glowing after being touched by the mist which had brought the monster to life. A desperate thought flashed across her mind. If she could dislodge the pin, maybe she could take that life away.

Zari stretched out her fingers and closed them around the gem. It felt surprisingly warm. Gasping for air, she yanked with all her strength. With a ripping sound, the gem came away in her hand.

The mummy's crushing embrace relaxed, and Zari sucked in a huge, unexpected breath. The iron grip on her wrist fell away as the mummy sank to the floor and lay still.

She stared in shock at the lifeless heap before her. The image of the fallen skeleton, separated from the gem on its helmet, filled her brain. Her thoughts whirling, she gazed at the gem in her hand. The light had vanished, leaving it dark and cold.

"A little help?" Mateo gasped, staring at her with bulging eyes. The second mummy held him against its chest, with one arm wrapped around his neck. A blue gem glowed ominously above Mateo's tangle of brown hair.

Zari lunged forward and tore the pin from the mummy's wrappings. The monster went slack and sank to the ground, taking Mateo with it.

She spun to find Taylor pressed against the wall, her flashlight and weapon at her feet. Taylor gripped the skeleton's wrist, straining to hold off the sword that inched its way toward her neck. The glow from the skeleton's helmet gem highlighted her desperate expression.

"Get rid of the gem!" Zari cried. She rushed forward and yanked the helmet from the skeleton's head. The bony warrior clattered to the floor, its sword clanging loudly against the stone.

Mateo scrambled away from the lifeless mummy with a shudder of revulsion. For a long moment, all three stared at one another, gasping for breath.

"It's . . . it's the gems," Zari said. "The blue mist touched the gems and woke them up, so we had to separate them from their . . . magic battery . . . or whatever."

Taylor nodded, her forehead shining with sweat. "Zari, that brain of yours annoys the snot out of me sometimes, but I'm loving it now." She cracked a smile. "We *can* beat them."

"At least we know how," Zari said, not quite as confident. She looked toward Mateo, and her excitement dimmed further when she saw his pained expression. "Are you hurt?"

Tears threatened to spill from Mateo's eyes. "I should have helped," he said, his voice strained.

"I froze when that first mummy grabbed your shoulder. And here . . . I curled up on the floor while you both fought. I'm . . . I'm such a coward."

Taylor's jaw dropped in surprise. They usually didn't talk about *those* kinds of feelings. Especially her. She looked down, probing the pile of bones with the tip of her shoe.

"That's not true," Zari said. "I mean, I'm not saying you're the bravest or anything, but you came through for me just now. You slashed that mummy right in the face. That was pretty awesome."

"And then I almost got choked out," he said miserably.

"That skeleton would have had me if it wasn't for Zari," Taylor said. "None of us are professional monster fighters. We all just did our best."

"And your best is good enough for us, okay?" Zari said.

Mateo stared at the floor, then nodded.

Taylor bent to pick up her flashlight and hooked weapon. Then she grabbed the skeleton's fallen sword and handed it to Zari. "Here. You earned this. Now you can get rid of that dumb baby club."

Wordlessly, Zari handed Taylor the helmet and took the sword. She'd never held one before. It felt heavy and awkward.

Taylor moved to set the helmet on the floor. Then she paused and slipped it onto her head.

"Wait, couldn't that gem control you, too?" Zari asked.

"Nah," Taylor said. "The light's out, and I'm not dead. Not yet, anyway."

She stepped over the lifeless mummies, and they all headed to Hezekiah's chamber.

This time, the vast burial room was empty, as the monsters roamed other parts of the weblike crypt.

"How do those skeletons see us?" Taylor mused. "They don't have eyes."

"And what if they wore glasses when they were alive?" Zari asked. "Does that mean they have blurry vision as skeletons?"

"Can't wear glasses now," Taylor said. "No ears."

Despite everything, Zari laughed. "We'd better hurry. No telling when the nasties will show up."

She grabbed a lit torch while Taylor and Mateo used their flashlights. They moved along the bone-decorated walls searching for an exit.

"Lots of crazy patterns, but nothing that looks like a door," Taylor said.

They came to a large tapestry of a man in a dark robe with his arms spread wide. Hundreds of people knelt before him.

"Do you think that's supposed to be Hezekiah?" Mateo asked.

"Delusional much?" Taylor said. "Talk about an ego trip."

After checking behind the tapestry for a hidden door, they climbed onto the platform. Zari was examining the huge pillars when Mateo grabbed her arm.

"Look!" he said in a harsh whisper.

Hezekiah's coffin was open.

CHAPTER 13

THEY STARED at the coffin in tense silence.

"I hope the skeletons did that," Taylor whispered.

They were too far away to see inside. "Is he . . . in there?" Mateo asked.

They inched forward, wanting to look in the coffin but afraid of what they'd find.

It was empty.

The coffin was lined with faded red silk, and beside the pillow stood a small, creepy statue of a cloaked figure with arms raised. *Why would someone* decorate a coffin? Zari wondered. *Maybe he wanted to be buried with some of his prized possessions.*

"Is the fact that it's empty good or bad?" Mateo asked.

They glanced at one another uneasily. "Let's keep moving," Zari said.

After searching the back wall, they descended the platform and continued working their way around the room.

"There's nothing here," Mateo said with a desperation they were all feeling. "We're never going to get out of this place."

They were examining the final section of wall beside an archway when a strange noise caught his ear. The sound echoed in the corridors, making it hard to pinpoint the source.

"Do you hear that?" he asked.

"It sounds like my dog when she runs," Taylor said. "Her claws click on the floor."

Mateo stiffened and caught the terrified look on Zari's face.

"Werewolf," he whimpered.

They flattened themselves against the wall as the werewolf burst from the nearby archway. He flew past without seeing them and slid to a stop in the center of the enormous room. Mateo had forgotten how huge he was, with coarse black hair and bulging muscles. Thanks to Taylor, the werewolf limped slightly. Slashes covered his chest and arms where the skeletons' swords had found their marks.

Before the werewolf turned around, Taylor grabbed Mateo's arm and pulled him into a new corridor, with Zari hurrying quietly after them.

As they slipped away, a tooth-rattling howl rang out. "Run!" Zari yelled, but Taylor and Mateo were already sprinting up the corridor.

They approached the central hub of the mummy chamber with the werewolf's howls echoing wildly behind them. One of the animated corpses blocked their path. Taylor raced by before it could react. The mummy made a grab for Mateo, but he slammed into its outstretched arm, causing it to spin aside. Zari slowed long enough to yank the blue gem from its chest, then continued into the chamber.

The mummy collapsed in front of the pursuing werewolf, causing him to stumble. As a second mummy moved to follow the friends, it lumbered into the werewolf's path. With a snarl of rage, he slashed out. The mummy pitched forward in the archway, its back shredded from shoulder to hip.

Zari ran across the web-patterned floor toward the spider statue in the center of the room. Another mummy tried to block her from following the others out the far side. Without thinking, she grabbed a handful of gold coins from the statue's bowl and threw them into the mummy's face. The monster staggered backward as the statue began to sink.

"Jump!" Taylor screamed from an archway.

Reacting on instinct, Zari leaped clear of the spiderweb pattern. As she landed, metal spikes four feet tall shot up from the floor behind her, one from each of the strange holes that dotted the web. As the spikes slammed into place, they heard the crunch of broken glass, and blue mist oozed from the holes. One of the spikes stuck the mummy right in the crotch, pinning it in place. It fell forward with a groan, clutching its privates.

"Ewww," Zari said.

"*That* had to hurt," said Taylor.

Mateo turned away with a grimace.

A forest of deadly spikes now filled the center of the mummy room. Across the chamber, the werewolf stood behind the new barrier and howled in frustration.

Taylor grabbed Zari's arm and pulled her through an archway. "Looks like you were right about those coins."

They raced up the corridor and back into the necromancy lab. They shut the door and wedged the chair under the handle. Before they reached their hiding place in the storage cabinet, the door shuddered under a tremendous impact. At the next blow, it flew open, snapping the chair into kindling. The werewolf burst into the room with a savage roar.

Faint with terror, they scrambled behind a table, trying to keep it between them and the monster. The werewolf froze Zari with his piercing gaze, the blue gem on his necklace swinging hypnotically. Razor-sharp fangs glinted in the torchlight as his face broke into an evil grin.

Knowing they were trapped, he moved leisurely now, like a monstrous cat playing with doomed mice. He herded them toward one end of the room, never allowing them a clear path to the exit. They huddled together as the werewolf leaped onto the table and stalked toward them.

With a strangled cry, Mateo jumped forward and slashed with his knife. The werewolf dodged, and the weapon barely grazed his leg. He lashed out with a kick that caught Mateo in the chest and sent him sliding across the floor. His head cracked against the stone wall, and he lay still.

Seeing her friend attacked filled Zari with a rage that burned away her fear. She glared up at the monster on the table, his gem necklace glittering tantalizingly out of reach. Rushing forward, she jammed her lit torch against his stomach. A sizzling sound filled the air followed by the noxious odor of burnt hair. The werewolf sprang back with a howl of pain.

Zari stood her ground, brandishing the torch. The monster moved forward cautiously, picking his way slowly across the table on all fours. With a quick lunge, he smacked the torch from her grip. She raised her sword clumsily, unused to the heavy weapon. The werewolf struck again, and his claws raked her forearm. She screamed and dropped the sword.

Defenseless, Zari turned toward Taylor.

She was gone.

The werewolf shot forward. A low, menacing growl rumbled beside Zari's ear. Trembling so hard she could barely stand, she turned to face him.

The werewolf's long muzzle was inches from her face. She felt his hot breath against her cheek and almost gagged on the odor of rotten meat. What had he eaten? A mummy? Hezekiah? Her stomach churned. His tongue lolled from his mouth, and a thick glob of saliva dripped onto her shoulder.

Zari gazed into the monster's blood-red eyes and waited for the end.

CHAPTER 14

WITH A maniacal yell, Taylor landed on the werewolf's back. He reared up in surprise, but she clung to his shoulders like she was riding the mechanical bull at Rowdy Red's BBQ Palace. The monster reached back to grab her. Just as his razor-sharp claws touched her skin, Zari ripped the golden chain from his neck, sending a few broken links plinking across the floor.

The werewolf froze.

Zari stared in shock as the monster turned back to stone, this time in a new and improved action pose. For a moment, no one moved. Taylor still clung to the werewolf's back, breathing heavily and clutching the dangling gem.

"You did it!" Zari cried.

Taylor slid down the statue's back and jumped unsteadily to the floor. Now that the threat of immediate death had passed, she felt a flood of dizziness wash over her. Had she really just jumped on a werewolf?

"I crawled under the table when Mateo attacked," Taylor said. "Then I moved behind Wolfy when you burned him."

"And saved my life. Again. Thank you."

"You saved my butt with that skeleton, so let's call it even. How's your arm?"

Zari had forgotten her injury in the shock of the moment. Now the pain came rushing back. Four gashes ran across her forearm, bleeding freely. "It hurts, but I'll live. Unless I get rabies."

"At least he didn't bite you. I don't need you going all wolfy on me every full moon."

A low groan made them both turn.

"Mateo!" Taylor said as they rushed over to him. "Are you okay?"

He pushed himself into a sitting position and rubbed his chest. "I'm stuck in a monster pit and just got body-slammed by a werewolf. So no."

"You were really brave to attack that thing," Taylor said. "A coward wouldn't have done that."

"Maybe," Mateo said, then looked up at the frozen werewolf. "I saw what you did. That was legendary."

"Couldn't have done it without you distracting him. In fact, here." She held out the gem necklace. "A souvenir to remind you of the time you attacked a werewolf."

"I think my nightmares will remind me plenty, but thanks," he said, slipping the necklace into his pocket.

Taylor closed the lab door. The chair they'd used to block it was in pieces, but at least they weren't visible to anything stalking the corridor. She bandaged Zari's arm with a roll of mummy wrappings. Zari didn't enjoy looking like the things that hunted them, but it stopped the bleeding.

Taylor rested her forehead against the cool stone wall and realized she could barely stand. When had she last eaten? Or slept? How long had they been trapped down here? It felt like a week. Wordlessly, she slid to the floor beside Zari and Mateo.

The mood turned heavy. The three friends sat silently, each of them processing the bitter reality of their situation in their own way.

"I wish my dad was here," Mateo said softly.

"And my mom," Taylor said. "She doesn't back down from anything."

Though Zari couldn't imagine her business-suit-wearing parents fighting in the crypt, she wished they were there with her anyway.

But the friends were alone. No one knew where they were. No one was coming. If they were going to survive, it was up to them.

"We can't just give up," Taylor said. But her heart wavered. Every passage they'd seen either sloped down to the coffin chamber or up to the stairs. There didn't seem to be a way out.

The reality of being truly trapped brought a fresh wave of fear crashing over Zari. Yet the thought of searching the monster-prowled corridors for an exit made her want to pretend she was safe in bed. She closed her eyes and took a few deep breaths. Pretending wasn't going to fix this mess. *Come on, brain! How can we survive this?* She waited for an idea to come, but nothing did. *I need more information. Where can I get it?*

Her eyes popped open. The journal. On their last trip to the lab, they'd had to leave before she'd finished reading it. Zari stood up and moved to where it lay on the table. She turned the thick pages, yellowed with age.

Taylor came up beside her. "Finding anything?"

Zari shook her head, continuing to scan pages. "Wait. Here's something: *The magic is more powerful than I'd hoped and more difficult than I'd imagined. I need time to master it, but that is the one resource that eludes me. I am growing old. I fear my goal is forever beyond my reach.*"

She turned the page. "Listen to this: *I found it! The Restoration Spell is the answer to my problem. It will extend my life far beyond its normal limits, giving me the precious time I need to build my army. Yet it comes at a cost—I must enter a hibernation-like state for an unknown period of time, perhaps even years. But no matter. What are a few years when I hold the key to eternity?"*

"Does that say what I think it says?" asked Mateo. "Is Hezekiah not dead?"

"Of course he's dead," said Taylor, not sounding completely confident. "We saw his coffin. And he was already old when he disappeared a hundred years ago. He'd be impossibly ancient by now."

"By normal standards, yeah," Zari said. "But if this Restoration Spell actually worked . . ."

They fell into an uncomfortable silence.

Taylor was the first to break it. "That's cool-yet-terrifying info, but what do we know that actually helps get us out of here?"

Zari tugged at one of her coils. "How many

creatures are left? The werewolf's out. And there were five skeletons to start."

"You and Wolfy both got one," Taylor said, "so that leaves three."

"There were eight mummies," Zari continued. "We took out two in that passage, and three more when we were being chased by the werewolf."

"Taylor cut one's hand off, but that doesn't mean it's down for good," Mateo said. "So there could still be three."

"And we don't know what happened to Hezekiah's body," Taylor said. "If he was in that coffin, where'd he go?" She sighed. "That's a lot of nasties left."

The mention of Hezekiah triggered something in Zari's brain. Something she'd seen. It felt important, but wiggled annoyingly out of reach.

"What about going back to the bookcase door?" she asked. "I know the werewolf shut it, but there must be a way to open it from this side."

"I couldn't find one when I was stuck there," Mateo said, "but it's worth another try."

They retrieved their weapons. Zari took a torch from the wall, deciding it was more important to have a light source and an additional weapon than to stay hidden.

They slipped out, moving quickly but quietly, their senses on high alert. Taylor led them up the corridor to the wide passageway, then peered around the corner toward the stairs.

"All clear," she whispered.

At the base of the steps, they found the remains of two skeleton warriors, their helmets and swords lying nearby.

"Looks like Wolfy got another one," Mateo said. "That means two skeletons left."

He and Taylor traded their weapons for swords, and they all climbed the stairs to the closed bookcase door.

"One of us should keep watch," Taylor said.

Mateo swallowed nervously. "I'll do it. I've already tried this." He went to the bottom of the staircase while Zari and Taylor looked for a way to open the door.

Minutes slipped by, but they found only wood, metal, and stone. Pushing, pulling, and twisting everything in sight yielded no results.

"Maybe I can pry it open," Taylor said.

She tried to wedge her sword into the crack around the doorframe, but the blade was too thick. She began hacking desperately at the heavy wood, but it was hardened with age and reinforced with iron bands. Her sword left dents and scratches without doing any real damage. The noise echoed loudly down the enclosed stairwell.

"Stop it!" Mateo whispered harshly up the steps. "That's going attract a lot of attention."

She huffed in frustration. "Do you have a better idea?"

"No, but I'm stuck down here protecting us, and you're ringing a dinner bell over my head!"

Zari rolled her eyes. "Everybody take a breath."

After a few tense moments, Mateo said, "What about the torch? Can you burn through the door?"

Zari's eyes widened in alarm. "Burn it? Did you think that idea through?"

Mateo shrugged. "Everything else is made of stone, so it's not like the fire could spread."

Conceding the point, Zari held the flames against the door until a sharp, smoky odor filled the tight space. When she pulled the torch away, there was only a blackened scorch on the smooth wood.

Defeated, Zari and Taylor slumped to the steps. Mateo joined them, his stomach growling loudly.

They slipped into silence. Zari realized that even if they survived until the ride opened in the morning, no one would hear them yelling. She had barely heard Mateo when she was beside the fireplace, and the car tracks were on the other side of the library. Not to mention the ride's music would be playing.

The desperation of their situation smothered Zari like a blanket. She thought about her parents. They'd never know what had happened to their only child. Her face flushed with anger at the thought. She couldn't let that happen. She *had* to escape.

The feeling that she'd forgotten something important tickled her brain again. Something she'd just been thinking about brought it back. What was it?

It came to her in a flash. Zari gasped and turned to the others.

"I think I might know a way out."

CHAPTER 15

"ARE YOU sure about this?" Taylor asked when Zari explained her idea.

"No," she admitted. "But it's the only thing I can think of."

"It's better than sitting here waiting for the next wave of creeps to come along," Mateo said, his leg bouncing. "Besides, I've gotta pee."

"You could use one of the jars in the necro lab," Taylor said.

"It might come to that."

Zari ground her teeth. Exhaustion, fear, and thirst were making her cranky. "A little focus, please? Taylor, lead the way."

At the bottom of the steps, Taylor looked around carefully, then slipped into the passageway. As they rounded a skull column, Taylor stiffened. A pair of blue gems glowing in the darkness surged toward them. The friends turned and ran down another corridor.

The sounds of pursuit grew louder. They burst into the mummy chamber and slid to a stop. A mummy blocked one of the downward corridors, bellowing loudly at them. The slap of bony feet echoed up the other passages to Hezekiah's burial chamber. They were being hemmed in fast. Taylor faced her friends with a scared but determined expression. With her sword and the skeleton's helmet, she looked like a young Amazon warrior.

She grabbed Zari's torch and handed her the flash-light. "You need time," she said quickly. "Keep the lights off and hide behind the mummy beds. When I lead them away, you two get to Hezekiah's chamber."

"But we don't split up!" Mateo cried.

"Find the way out!" Taylor said fiercely. "I'll meet up with you!" She turned and raced toward the mummy who stood waiting for reinforcements. Jumping onto one of the stone mummy beds, she launched herself at the monster with a scream of rage.

"No!" Zari cried as the mummy opened its arms to catch Taylor in a crushing embrace. But Zari had forgotten Taylor had a case full of gymnastics trophies. She twisted in midair and slammed her foot into the mummy's chest. It staggered backward and fell onto the spiderweb of waist-high spikes in the center of the room. Two metal tips emerged from its chest, completely impaling it. The mummy didn't seem to be in pain, but it writhed wildly, unable to free itself.

As her friends gaped, Taylor turned and hissed, "Hide!" Then she ran up a corridor toward the staircase, shouting loudly and waving her torch. Zari pulled Mateo down just before the two remaining skeletons and two mummies poured into the chamber. They raced after Taylor, following the light and noise.

"She . . . she shouldn't have done that," Mateo whispered.

"I know." Zari wavered, wondering if they should try to help their friend. But she knew what Taylor wanted. "Come on. Let's not waste the chance she gave us."

Zari took the lead, trying not to think of what might happen to Taylor. They clicked on their flashlights as they ran through an archway, leaping over the crumpled mummies they'd fought earlier. They continued down the sloping corridor until they reached Hezekiah's burial chamber.

They hurried across the vast empty room and onto the platform, then stopped at the abandoned coffin, breathing hard. Now that the moment had come, Zari thought her idea seemed ridiculous.

"Go ahead," said Mateo. "Try it."

She stared down at the small statue standing near the coffin's pillow. The one she'd noticed earlier. The one that didn't make sense in a casket. It looked similar to the statue on the mantel that triggered the secret door in the library. Taking a deep breath, she reached out and pushed it over.

With a soft click, the bottom half of the coffin floor dropped away, revealing a circular stone staircase leading down into darkness.

"You were right!" Mateo cried. "You found a way out!"

Zari drew a shuddering breath, relief flooding through her. Then she hesitated. "Maybe. We don't know where it leads or what else is down there. And going further underground isn't helpful."

"But maybe nothing will follow us, so at least we'll solve one problem," Mateo said. His eyes were red-rimmed and brimming, like he was about to break down.

Zari looked anxiously at the empty archways across the chamber. There was no sign of Taylor. She bit her lip.

Two agonizingly long minutes passed.

Finally, Zari said, "We have to go after her."

Mateo paused for a moment, then nodded, looking fearful but resolved.

They ran down the platform steps and across the huge chamber. As they reached an exit, a voice called out behind them. Taylor burst from a passageway and staggered toward them, her face streaked with sweat.

"Taylor!" Mateo cried as they ran to her. She collapsed in his arms, breathing in huge gasps.

"Are you okay?" Zari asked anxiously.

"No," she wheezed. "I really gotta pee."

"Zari found the way out!" Mateo said.

"Maybe," Zari said. "We haven't tried it yet."

"What are we waiting for?" Taylor said. "Let's go before our friends come back."

As Mateo and Taylor turned toward the platform, Zari glanced back at the empty corridors and thought they just might survive this after all.

Then Mateo gasped.

"Duckweed," Taylor said with a deep sigh. "I forgot about her."

Zari whirled. Towering in front of the coffin was the lizard creature.

And she wasn't a statue anymore.

CHAPTER 16

THE SEVEN-FOOT monster's dark green scales glinted dully in the torchlight. She flexed her thick fingers slowly, brandishing hooked claws. Catfish-like feelers waved like miniature snakes around her blunt muzzle. Her bulging eyes blinked lazily as if she had all the time in the world to kill them.

"Help," Mateo whimpered.

"Get her necklace off," Taylor said quietly.

"Or slip past her into the coffin," Zari said. "She might not fit down the stairs."

The lizard woman stalked down the platform steps, her long tail swishing casually. A blood-red forked tongue flitted between her protruding fangs.

"Spread out," Taylor whispered. "When she goes for one of us, the other two attack from behind."

Mateo and Zari stepped tentatively away from Taylor. Her plan made sense, but separating made them feel more vulnerable. Zari held out her trembling sword.

The lizard woman reached the chamber floor and approached Taylor, her huge round eyes flicking back and forth to track the others. Taylor crouched, her sword in one hand and torch in the other. Taking the offensive, she lunged forward and pressed her burning torch against the monster's stomach like Zari had done with the werewolf.

The lizard woman stood motionless.

Taylor's face went slack in surprise. "Uh-oh."

The monster ripped the torch from Taylor's hand and tossed it aside. Her midsection was completely unharmed by the fire, as if her scales were like dragon armor. She lowered her head to stare directly into Taylor's face. They all froze, hypnotized by the unexpected behavior. The monster released a dry, menacing hiss.

The sound broke Zari's paralysis. She ran forward with a strangled cry and swung her sword at the lizard woman's head. The monster raised her arm and blocked the blow. Zari felt like she'd struck concrete. Impact vibrations ran up her arms, and she yelped as her sword clattered to the floor. The lizard woman regarded Zari for a moment with her yellow eyes, flexing the uninjured arm. Then she thrust her hand into Zari's shoulder and sent her sliding across the floor.

Taylor drove the point of her sword into the monster's side. The blade didn't penetrate, but she was rewarded with a satisfying grunt from the lizard woman.

"Mateo, come on!" Taylor yelled.

Her cry shocked him into action. Mateo ran forward with his sword in both hands over his head. The monster whipped her muscular tail into his feet, and he flipped up like he was on roller skates. Mateo landed with a crunch on the tile floor and lay groaning.

The lizard woman stalked Taylor in a slow circle. Taylor crouched low with her sword raised, shuffling her feet to keep the monster in front of her. Zari massaged her aching shoulder as she stood and retrieved her weapon. Taylor gave her friend a quick nod, her expression grim but focused. Zari moved behind the lizard woman as Taylor jabbed with her sword, keeping the monster's attention.

The golden chain glimmered against the back of the lizard woman's neck. Taking a deep breath, Zari raced forward and stretched out her sword to snag the necklace.

Without turning, the monster thrust her leg back and caught Zari squarely in the stomach. She dropped to her knees near Taylor's fallen torch and gasped for breath like a beached fish.

Taylor darted in and jabbed at the monster's face, but the lizard woman knocked the blow aside with lightning reflexes. She seemed to be enjoying the game and was in no hurry to end it.

"Zari, Mateo, get out of here," Taylor called, her eyes never leaving her opponent. "Go down the coffin stairs."

Mateo pulled himself painfully to his feet. "But what about you?"

"Get help," she said. "I'll follow if I can."

Zari was finally able to suck in a ragged breath. "Can't . . . leave you."

"Do it!" Taylor yelled. "This thing's too strong. It's our only chance."

Mateo gave a reluctant nod, then ran up the steps toward the coffin. Zari swayed unsteadily, agonizing over whether to follow him or help Taylor.

The decision was made for her. The lizard woman whirled and made an incredible leap to the top of the platform. She plucked Mateo up by the shoulders and held him off the ground. His face locked in a silent scream as she pulled him toward her, so close that her flicking tongue caressed his cheek. Horrified but unable to look away, he gazed into the monster's hypnotic eyes like a bird trapped before a cobra.

Carrying Mateo back down the steps, the lizard woman unceremoniously stuffed him butt-first into the mouth of one of the large urns beside the stage. His nose was jammed against his knees with his sneakers pointing toward the ceiling.

The monster turned and began circling Taylor, obviously finding her to be the most entertaining opponent. Zari growled in fear and frustration. The lizard woman seemed nearly invincible and clearly wasn't letting them go. The only way out of this was to get her necklace. Whatever happened, Zari couldn't let Taylor face this overgrown gecko alone.

Ignoring the protests of her aching body, Zari picked up her sword. Then as she stepped forward, something grabbed her from behind in a crushing embrace.

"Ugh!" she cried. "Not another stupid mummy!"

The mummy's roughly wrapped arms held her in an iron grip. Zari tried to grab its hands to pry them apart but found there was only one. She touched the dry stump where Taylor's blade had done its work, then snatched her hand away. No matter how hard she struggled, she couldn't break free.

Turning her head, Zari saw the glowing gem on the mummy's chest, but with her arms pinned, she couldn't reach it. Straining her neck, she tried grabbing the gem with her teeth, but it was too far away. The mummy tightened its grip, and Zari felt faint as her lungs fought to expand. She felt a strange heat on the back of her legs, and the small part of her mind not consumed with breathing realized what it was—Taylor's fallen torch, still burning brightly.

Her oxygen-starved brain latched on to a final, desperate idea. Still locked in the mummy's embrace, Zari wrapped her right leg behind its knee and yanked it forward, while kicking her left foot against the side of the platform steps. The unexpected move pushed the mummy off-balance, and unable to recover, it fell backward onto the flaming torch.

Blazing heat toasted Zari's skin as fire erupted around her. For a terrifying moment, she thought she would burn with the mummy. Finally, its crushing grip relaxed. As the flames swept over the dry wrappings, she rolled away, frantically slapping at her smoldering clothes.

The mummy rose and staggered around like a stuntperson on a movie set. Then the blue gem tumbled free of the burning cloth and the mummy collapsed, lifeless once more.

"At least *they* burn," Zari muttered as she sat up, breathing heavily.

The lizard woman was still toying with Taylor, who kept trying new, unsuccessful ways to get the monster's gem. With a small popping sound, Mateo pulled himself free from the urn. Zari felt sorry for him. They'd all taken a beating, but being stuck butt-first in an urn was just plain humiliating.

The clattering of feet echoed across the burial chamber. A skeleton warrior appeared in a corner archway and raced toward them. Then a second skeleton ran in from the opposite corner. Mateo, his shirt torn and his hair sticking out wildly, watched them approach with wide, bloodshot eyes.

"You take that one . . ." Zari began, but stopped when she saw the look on Mateo's face. He stared frantically around the room, his chest rising and falling rapidly. He turned to her with a wretched expression and shook his head.

"I can't do this anymore," he said, trembling. Then he turned and sprinted toward the center exit.

"Matty, wait!" Zari cried.

The lizard woman flicked her eyes in his direction, but made no move to stop him. Apparently, she knew he was still trapped like a rat in a cage. As he disappeared through the archway, one of the skeletons veered off to follow him.

A sob escaped Zari's chest. She couldn't believe it.

Mateo had abandoned them.

CHAPTER 17

TAYLOR GROWLED angrily—she'd seen Mateo leave. But Zari didn't have time for anger or sadness. The remaining skeleton charged her with frightening speed. She turned and fled toward the far side of the room, desperately wondering how she could fight this bonehead on her own.

When Zari reached the wall, she still had no plan. She ducked. The skeleton's sword swept over her head and clanged against the stone. Crying out, she scrambled left, realizing too late that she'd worked her way into a corner. The skeleton quickly moved to trap her.

Zari stood with her back pressed against the wall and her sword held tightly in front of her. She clenched her teeth, her adrenaline surging. There was no one to help her now. She had to face this nightmare alone.

The skeleton pressed the attack, darting in to stab at her waist. Zari clumsily deflected the strike, then slashed back, but her attempt went wide. The skeleton swung its sword in an arc. She managed to block it, but the force of the blow was too much. Her sword flew from her hands and spun away.

Defenseless now, she stared into her attacker's empty eye sockets. With a howl, she leaped forward and jabbed her fingers into the holes in the skull.

Nothing happened.

"How can you see me?" Zari screamed in its face. She tried to knock its helmet off before she retreated, but the skeleton jerked away. Her heart hammered in her chest, and her panicked mind was blank. When the monster rushed in for another attack, she acted on instinct. Dropping to her knees, she dove forward between its legs. Scrambling to her feet, Zari raced toward the stage, followed by the slap of bone on stone.

After pulling herself up the side of the chest-high platform, she glanced at the coffin, wondering if she could escape, or at least use it as a barrier. The lizard woman stopped her with an icy gaze. The monster wouldn't let her get too close to freedom.

The skeleton swept its blade at Zari's feet, forcing her to jump awkwardly. As it hooked its elbows onto the platform to climb after her, inspiration struck. Zari leaped forward and landed on its sword arm, pinning it to the platform. Then she reached down and yanked the helmet from its skull.

The skeleton froze momentarily, then tumbled to the floor in a pile of bones.

"Way to go, girl!" Taylor called. "Now get over here and help me!"

Zari glanced toward the doorway Mateo had taken and hesitated. She was furious with him for leaving, but what if he needed help too? Then she clenched her jaw. There was nothing she could do for him now. Grabbing the skeleton's sword, Zari ran down the steps to stand beside Taylor. As fierce as she was, the battle was clearly taking its toll. Taylor's arms drooped, and she struggled to keep her sword point off the floor.

She gave Zari an exhausted glance, her face shining with sweat. "I'm really sorry about all this."

"Me too," Zari wheezed back, her own limbs trembling with fear and weariness. She lifted her sword.

"Ready?" Taylor asked.

"Does it matter?"

"Nope."

They were about to make a last desperate grab for the necklace when a dry hiss from the lizard woman chilled their blood. The monster spun and slammed her tail into their legs, knocking them over like bowling pins. Taylor's helmet flew from her head and clattered across the tiles.

The lizard woman darted forward and yanked their swords away. She tossed them aside, then placed her huge feet across their legs. They cried out as the monster's crushing weight pinned them to the floor. She towered over them with a fearsome expression, her necklace dangling hopelessly out of reach.

The game was over.

Taylor's throat clenched in despair. She couldn't speak, couldn't breathe. With her eyes locked on the horrifying face above her, she reached out and found Zari's hand. She squeezed it and felt her friend's grip in return.

With a look of triumph, the lizard woman raised her clawed hand for the final strike.

CHAPTER 18

THE BLOW didn't come.

The lizard woman paused, her gaze now fixed on an archway. Her tongue flicked in and out, tasting the air.

Then the squeak of sneakers echoed down a corridor.

Seconds later, Mateo burst into the chamber, arms flailing, feet flying as he hurtled toward them. His expression was a mix of exhaustion and sheer terror.

The werewolf exploded from the archway, close on Mateo's heels. Taylor gaped at the monster in horror and confusion. They'd left him frozen as a statue in the lab. Somehow the life-giving pendant was back around the werewolf's neck, its broken chain tied in a knot. The gem glowed brightly as it bounced against his chest.

Mateo raced straight toward them as the werewolf closed the gap and reached out to grab him. As Mateo drew close, the lizard woman swiped at his head. He dove to one side, and the monster's claws swept over him.

And into the face of the charging werewolf.

The werewolf howled in pain and fury. He slammed into the lizard woman, sending her crashing to the floor. Now free, Zari and Taylor scrambled up and limped away on numb legs with Mateo.

The two monsters wrestled wildly, slashing and biting each other. The werewolf strained to clamp his jaws on the lizard woman's throat, but she dug her claws into his chest, holding him at bay. With a menacing hiss, she wrapped her tail around his waist and squeezed like a boa constrictor. The werewolf grunted and raked his claws across her stomach, leaving long furrows in her scales.

Gasping for breath, Mateo pulled Taylor and Zari toward the platform. "We . . . gotta . . . go."

Taylor tore her eyes from the titanic struggle. They stumbled up the steps and over to the coffin. Zari climbed in, then stepped down onto the hidden staircase. Mateo and Taylor quickly followed. Taylor tried to lift the bottom of the coffin back into place, but it wouldn't budge.

The circular staircase was steep and narrow, and they fought to keep their footing on the slick stone. After descending fifteen steps, they came to a dark tunnel. The torchlight filtering through the open casket barely reached them.

"We need light," Zari whispered.

Mateo groaned. In all the running and fighting in the burial chamber, they'd dropped their flashlights. None of them had thought to grab a light or a sword.

"I . . . I could go back," Zari said, though she wasn't sure if she could force herself.

"No way!" Mateo said.

"But how are we going to manage the tunnel without light?" Taylor asked.

Zari rubbed her temples, thinking furiously. "By feel. We'll lock hands and keep touching the side walls."

"Those things can't fit through the coffin, right?" Mateo asked anxiously.

A shadow blocked out the dim light above them, followed by the sound of a heavy tread on the stairs. Mateo seized Taylor's arm as his heart rocketed into his throat.

Just before they ran blindly into the tunnel, they heard an unusually high-pitched moan. Then, an irregular thumping sound grew steadily louder and thumpier. A few seconds later, a mummy somer-saulted out of the staircase and landed in a groan-ing heap at their feet.

"Dude," said Mateo.

Taylor casually reached down and tore the blue gem from the mummy's chest. "Clumsy little sucker."

"At least he didn't have his butt stuck in an urn," Mateo said.

After lining up, they headed into the inky black-ness of the tunnel. Taylor and Mateo kept their outer hands on the cool stone walls with Zari in the middle. She felt weird holding hands with Mateo, especially after he had bailed on them. Her stom-ach twisted uncomfortably at the thought of con-fronting him, and she almost left it for Taylor. Then she remembered her promise to speak up. She'd avoided starting hard conversations long enough.

"So . . . what happened back there, Mateo?" Zari asked, her voice tight. "You . . . you kind of ditched us when those skeletons came in."

She felt him tense in the darkness. "I know, but . . ." Mateo began, then paused. As much as he wanted to make excuses, he knew he should tell the truth. His shoulders slumped. "Yeah, I lost it. I mean, I was terrified and pretty roughed up, but so were both of you. I'm *really* sorry. I knew there was no way we were going to beat that lizard lady, and she wasn't going to let us go either. When the skeletons came in, it was too much, so I just . . . ran." He blew out a long breath. "But when I got to the lab, I came around and wanted to help. I saw the werewolf statue and . . . had an idea."

Taylor, who'd been squeezing Zari's hand angrily

while Mateo spoke, softened her grip. "Wait. Do you mean *you* woke up the werewolf?"

"It was probably really stupid," he said. "But I had the necklace in my pocket, and it was the only thing I could think of. I figured if I could get him to chase me, I could lead him to the lizard lady. Maybe he'd fight her like he did the skeletons, and we'd have a chance to get away. I put the necklace on him and opened one of the vials of blue mist. Then I ran like a rabbit."

"Wow," Zari said, reluctantly impressed. "That was gutsy."

"And super risky," Taylor said. "But brave. I guess I'm glad you ditched us long enough to think of that. You definitely can't call yourself a coward now. You really saved our butts."

They walked in silence for a while, thinking about all the unbelievable things they'd experienced since entering Grimstone Manor. And they weren't free yet.

"There's not, like, spiders or anything down here, right?" Mateo asked.

"Nah," Taylor said. "I'm sure the maid came through this morning."

In the stifling darkness, Zari struck her forehead on something hard. "Ow!"

"What happened?" Taylor asked anxiously.

"Hit my head," Zari said irritably, pulling her hand from Mateo's to probe the injury. She reached out blindly and felt a rock jutting down. "Low ceiling. I need one hand free to hold in front of me while we walk. Mateo, put your hand on my waist."

"Yeah," he said, "'cause that's not awkward or anything."

"I'll do it," Taylor said.

Zari felt a hand grab her butt. "Whoa, a little low there."

"How are you so tall?" Taylor said, snickering.

And then they all laughed—the bent-over, hysterical kind of laughter that you get when you're exhausted and you almost died and then a mummy fell down the stairs and everything is inexplicably hilarious.

Finally, they pulled themselves together and continued shuffling down the dark tunnel. A few minutes later, Zari's outstretched hand hit something solid.

"Stop," she said. "There's something here."

"Another rock?" Mateo asked.

She slid her hand over the obstruction. "No. Smoother, like wood." Her fingers brushed what felt like a metal band. "I think it's a door." She moved her hand over to the doorframe, then followed it down. "I've got the handle!"

"Open it!" cried Mateo.

Zari turned the handle and pulled. The door creaked slowly open.

CHAPTER 19

THERE WAS nothing. At least it looked like nothing. Unbroken darkness lay on the other side of the door.

"Unbelievable," Mateo said bitterly.

"There's gotta be something," Zari said. "This door is here for a reason."

She shuffled forward until her hand bumped into cool, smooth stone with a curved shape. "There's, like, a pillar or something. Check for candles. There could be matches!" Their search came up empty, but Zari's groping hands found a flat horizontal surface with a second one above it. "I think it's another spiral staircase, and it's leading up!"

"Now we're talking!" Taylor said. She reached out, exploring the steps with her hands. "We'll have to go single file. I'll go first. Zar, put your hand on my shoulder, and, Matty, hold the back of her shirt."

They awkwardly arranged themselves in the cramped space, then slowly ascended, feeling for each step with their feet. It was disorienting to move blindly upward in a spiral. As the seconds crawled by, Mateo imagined how ridiculous they would look if anyone could see them.

After what felt like a long climb, Taylor said, "Hold up. There's something above my head."

"Is there a handle or anything?" Mateo asked, his voice floating up through the darkness.

"I don't think so," she said.

"Try pushing up on it," Zari said. "Maybe it's a trapdoor."

Taylor grunted. "Not . . . moving. Zari, come help me."

Zari carefully squeezed in beside her, then reached up and felt the smooth surface. She crouched and turned to face down the staircase, then cautiously stood until her shoulder blades touched the wood. "Okay, on three. One, two, three!"

Zari heaved upward with her legs as Taylor pushed with her hands. The wood creaked and lifted a few inches. Soft light streamed in, and they squinted after spending so long in absolute darkness. A smattering of dirt and leaves fell onto the steps, and a fresh breeze kissed their faces. They kept pushing, and the trapdoor fell open.

Scrambling eagerly out of the hole, they found themselves in a dark wooded area between two rides. Light from the amusement park filtered in through the trees.

"We made it out!" Mateo exclaimed, his voice thick with emotion.

Zari bent forward and grabbed her knees, nearly buckling in relief. She couldn't believe it. The horror was finally over. They were free. Taylor pulled Zari and Mateo into a spontaneous group hug as tears of relief ran down their faces.

When they finally separated, Zari examined the trapdoor. It was hinged on one side and tilted back, propped up by a bush fastened to its top. She lowered it into place.

"That's wild," said Taylor. "The opening completely disappears. You'd never know it was there."

"Somebody went to a lot of trouble to hide it," Zari said.

It didn't matter to Mateo who that might be. He just wanted to go home. The menacing outline of Grimstone Manor rose above the trees, and his stomach twisted.

"Our phones are probably at the lost and found, but let's check the boathouse since we're close,"

Zari said. "If they're still in the locker, we can call our parents."

"We're gonna be so busted," Taylor said.

"I think once they hear the whole story," Mateo said, "they'll be too glad we're alive to punish us."

"If they believe us at all," Zari said wearily.

They wound through the trees and emerged next to a souvenir cart. "Hold up," Taylor said. She grabbed an I SURVIVED GRIMSTONE MANOR T-shirt from a rack and tossed it to Mateo.

"You can't just steal a shirt," Zari said, becoming more comfortable with speaking her mind.

"I got it," Taylor said, laying some money on the counter. "Mateo needs a new souvenir since he gave the necklace back to the werewolf. Besides, that grabby mummy ripped his shirt."

Exhausted, they limped through the ride entrance to the boathouse. The effects were turned off, but it was still creepy, especially with the hooded animatronic skeleton standing silently nearby. Even Taylor had seen enough skeletons for a lifetime.

"Let's make this quick," Mateo said uneasily.

Taylor hurried over to the lockers and pulled the key from her pocket. A moment later, she sighed. "They're gone."

"And the lost and found will be locked up," Mateo said. "We *cannot* catch a break here."

"We just have to find someone," Zari said. "They must have security guards at night."

"We'll get in trouble for being here after the park's closed," Taylor said.

"For once, I honestly don't care about getting in trouble," Mateo said.

They walked back through the eerily empty park. The attractions were dark and silent. It was strange being alone in a place that was normally so crowded.

They'd almost reached the exit before they finally found a guard. He was standing in the shadows with his back to them, gazing up at the night sky.

"Excuse me, sir?" Zari said.

If the man heard her, he gave no sign. They moved closer. "Um . . . hello?" Taylor asked. "Can you help us?"

The guard continued staring silently upward. The friends glanced at one another in confusion.

Then the man began to speak, low and soft in a language they didn't understand. His voice had a harsh, strained quality, yet was strangely compelling. Zari began to feel sleepy. Her eyelids grew heavy, and her mind felt sluggish. She glanced at Mateo and Taylor. They were both staring at the man with slack, glazed expressions. What was going on?

Finally, he turned toward them and stepped into the light. He wore a dark robe, and his gray face was scored with deep lines. A blue gem hung around his neck from a thin gold chain. It was no security guard.

It was Hezekiah Crawly.

CHAPTER 20

THE UNDEAD necromancer moved toward them, continuing his hypnotic incantation. Zari's arms felt like they were made of bowling balls. She was so tired. All she wanted to do was lie down.

Sleep, Hezekiah's voice whispered invitingly in her brain. *Sleep!*

Beside her, Taylor and Mateo slowly lowered themselves to the ground. *I should rest too,* Zari thought. *Just for a little while.*

But another part of her brain objected. *No, Zari! Don't do it!*

But why? she thought. *It would be so easy.*

Sleep! Hezekiah's voice came again to her mind, more urgent this time, more commanding. *You must sleep!*

"I . . . can't . . . sleep," she murmured, swaying unsteadily with her eyelids drooping.

Hezekiah moved toward her, his hand out-stretched. She could see the network of veins beneath his paper-thin skin and his curved, yellowish nails as he reached for her. He held a familiar-looking glass vial, but the mist inside was bright green. His blood-shot eyes glimmered, and his ancient, wrinkled face had the gray look of a corpse. The mind-numbing incantation continued in an unbroken stream. *Breathe,* his voice commanded as he lifted the vial to her face.

Don't . . . breathe it, Zari thought. *Must . . . wake . . . up.* She tried to pinch herself in the thigh, but her limp fingers closed on something in her pocket. It was hard and oddly shaped, like a small club. *The pestle.* Her mind seized on the strange word, and it anchored her thoughts.

With incredible effort, Zari pushed her hand into her pocket. Her fingers closed around the cool stone handle. Hezekiah held the vial beneath her nose and began to pull the stopper.

Breathe! his voice ordered in her mind as the green mist swirled eagerly in its container.

With her last reserve of strength, Zari yanked the stone pestle from her pocket and slammed it into Hezekiah's hand. The glass vial flew through the air and shattered on the pavement. Unlike the blue mist, which slithered like an airborne snake, the green mist simply floated away on the night breeze.

The necromancer cried out in surprise and anger. With the flow of his incantation broken, the fog over Zari's mind cleared. Her eyes snapped open as he reached for her throat. Instinctively, she swung the pestle up between his outstretched arms. The heavy stone struck the bottom of Hezekiah's chin with a crack, and he staggered backward.

With a scream of rage, Taylor sprang up and flew at Hezekiah like an enraged badger. The unexpected attack caught the necromancer off-balance, and he fell. Taylor straddled his chest and pinned him to the ground.

Mateo staggered over to help Taylor.

A long, bone-chilling howl rang out, followed by the rapid slap of padded feet on pavement. Everyone turned in the direction of the sound, staring in horror along the walkway leading back into the park.

The werewolf was coming.

Zari lurched forward and pulled her friends to their feet. "Run!"

They rushed to the nearby exit and threw themselves against the gates. Locked. Looking around desperately, Taylor spied a trash container near the high brick wall beside the exit.

"Follow me!" She climbed onto the container, then jumped up and caught the top of the wall. After pulling herself up, she lay on her stomach and reached down. Zari grabbed her hand and climbed nimbly up. Then, straining with effort, they both hauled Mateo to the top.

They glanced back at the moonlit walkway. Hezekiah was standing now, but he wasn't looking at them. He faced into the park. The werewolf, with the blue gem swinging freely around his neck, raced toward the man. Raising his arms, the necromancer rapidly began chanting an incantation.

It was too late. The monster snatched Hezekiah from his feet like a toy and held him up with a howl of triumph.

As the werewolf lowered the screaming necromancer to his open jaws, the three friends dropped over the wall and fled into the night.

ACKNOWLEDGMENTS

TO GOD for being my North Star.

To my wife, Lisa, the best mentor and writing coach ever! This book would not exist without your generosity, patience, and trailblazing tenacity. I love you.

To my kids, Kilian and Kennedy. You inspire me. Seeing you follow your dreams is even more fun than reaching my own.

To my parents for a house full of books and unconditional support of my artistic dreams. Your belief in me helped me believe in myself.

To Michael Bourret, the best agent and friend in the business. Thanks for taking a chance on me, for your unerring guidance, and for making room for a second McMann on your list!

To Jen Klonsky, publisher extraordinaire. Thank you for respecting me enough to say no to my first book so I could trust your yes on this one. Lisa partnered with you at the beginning of her journey—I'm thrilled I can say the same!

To Stephanie Pitts, the kind of editor authors dream of having! Your artistry, insight, professionalism, and kindness have made this book so much better and helped me navigate the debut maze in more ways than you know.

To Matt Phipps for fantastic admin skills, wonderful communication, great editorial advice, and general awesomeness.

To Ari Lewin for being the first editor to believe in this idea. I will always be grateful.

To Ryan Quickfall for bringing your illustrative genius to this project. You made a cover that would make me snatch up this book now as much as when I was a kid.

To Danielle Ceccolini for a wonderfully spooky cover design, Ana Deboo and Cindy Howle for spot-on copyediting, and to all the hardworking superstars in every department at Penguin Young Readers, including art, school & library, sales, marketing, and publicity. This is our book.

To Bob Douglas, my seventh and eighth grade English teacher, for being the first person to make me believe I could be an author.

To all the booksellers, librarians, teachers, book reviewers, and other adults who help kids find books that serve as mirrors and windows. What you do is essential, and we need you now more than ever. I am so grateful for how you've embraced me and this series!

To Bill Konigsberg, Tom Leveen, Kevin Sylvester, Sara Zarr, Barney Saltzberg, Kevin Sands, Aprilynne Pike, James Riley, James Owen, Jon Lewis, Kevin Emerson, Kim Baker, Susan Young, Alyson Noël, Anna-Marie McLemore, Amy King, Lisa Schmid, and so many others for tirelessly answering my endless questions on how to be an author. I will always be grateful.

To my #2023debut community for all your support and camaraderie through the debut trenches. I'm so glad for your company on this road!

To the stunningly talented authors who agreed to blurb this book. I'm still shocked and incredibly grateful.

To the myriad of authors whose books have inspired me and paved the way, including Lindsay Currie, Lorien Lawrence, Katherine Arden, Jonathan Stroud, and Alvin Schwartz. A special shout-out to R. L. Stine and Neil Gaiman for their brilliant MasterClasses and congratulatory tweets.

Finally, to you, my amazing readers. Without you, the monsters in these pages would only be haunting my dreams. Thank you for coming with me on this wild ride. I hope we go on many more spooky adventures together!

Photo © Kennedy McMann

As a professional musician, **Matt McMann** played an NFL stadium, a cruise ship, and the International Twins Convention. Now he writes the kind of spooky mystery-adventure books he loved as a kid. He's hiked the Pacific Northwest, cruised Loch Ness, and chased a ghost on a mountain. While he missed Bigfoot and Nessie, he caught the ghost. He enjoys brainstorming new books with his wife, *New York Times* bestselling author Lisa McMann; viewing his son Kilian McMann's artwork; and watching his daughter, actor Kennedy McMann, on television.

You can visit Matt at
MattMcMann.com

And follow him on Instagram and Twitter
@Matt_McMann

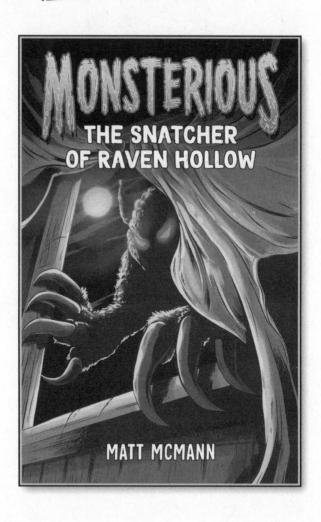